MW00459761

EVERY
SUMMER DAY

By the Author

My Aim Is True
Dreamspinner Press

Love and Genetic Weaponry: The Beginner's Guide
Alyson Books

Nothing Gold Can Stay (writing as Casey Nelson)
Alyson Books

Visit us at www.boldstrokesbooks.com

EVERY
SUMMER DAY

by

Lee Patton

Clearwater Public Library
100 N. Osceola Avenue
Clearwater, FL 33755

2020

EVERY SUMMER DAY

© 2020 By Lee Patton. All Rights Reserved.

ISBN 13: 978-1-63555-706-0

This Trade Paperback Original Is Published By
Bold Strokes Books, Inc.
P.O. Box 249
Valley Falls, NY 12185

First Edition: June 2020

THIS IS A WORK OF FICTION. NAMES, CHARACTERS, PLACES, AND INCIDENTS ARE THE PRODUCT OF THE AUTHOR'S IMAGINATION OR ARE USED FICTITIOUSLY. ANY RESEMBLANCE TO ACTUAL PERSONS, LIVING OR DEAD, BUSINESS ESTABLISHMENTS, EVENTS, OR LOCALES IS ENTIRELY COINCIDENTAL.

THIS BOOK, OR PARTS THEREOF, MAY NOT BE REPRODUCED IN ANY FORM WITHOUT PERMISSION.

CREDITS
EDITORS: JERRY L. WHEELER AND STACIA SEAMAN
PRODUCTION DESIGN: STACIA SEAMAN
COVER DESIGN BY TAMMY SEIDICK

Acknowledgments

Many thanks to Patricia Mosco Holloway and George Ware, my first readers; and to Jerry Wheeler for his meticulous diligence. Thanks also to Kristen Hannum and John Serini for editing assistance with the opening, and to Jean C. Smith for guiding us to Summitville Mine.

For George

AFTERWARD: DECEMBER 31

"So, how was the last one of the year?" Jenn asks him, closing her door gently for the baby's sake.

"Okay." Shrugging, Luke tries to smile. Face-to-face in the narrow hallway, they're aimed in different directions, Jenn downstairs to the party, Luke to his room to evade it. "It still feels weird to ski solo all day."

"I miss him, too. He used to ski with me all morning, then hit the expert terrain by himself in the afternoon."

"Same with me."

"Well, I'm going to hit the holiday leftovers. And maybe score some of your dad's spiked eggnog while the baby's napping. You coming downstairs?"

"Yeah," he lies. "Later."

They go quiet, listening to the party echoing in the stairwell—teasing, laughter, the clinks of wine goblets and eggnog cups.

"It's so good to hear your mom laugh again," Jenn says, smiling. "That loopy har-de-har of hers. Just like Matt's."

"Yeah. Good to have that ol' loopy har-de-har around the house again."

Luke slipped through the family party when he got home, hugging his dad, bussing his mom's cheek, and raising an empty hand to join a cousin's toast to the new year. Then, on the pretext he needed to get out of his ski gear, he hustled upstairs.

Now he's on pause in the hallway, and Jenn is smiling at him, easy in the silence that falls between them again. Lately, introducing her, Luke's taken to dropping the "in-law" from "sister." He always wanted a sister, and now he has one, living in his brother's old room. Ex-room. Jenn's room now.

"See ya down there."

"Save me some nog?"

The glare from the overhead bulb reveals every flaw in the hallway's century-old walls, the cracks and pockmarks paint can't hide anymore. Heading into his room, Luke leaves it dark. Under a window lit by streetlight, his desk taunts him with ungraded exams from Contemporary History, untouched every day of winter break. There's no more avoiding them. One very fat, very old orange tomcat broods over the stack as if trying to hatch more essays for Luke to grade.

Climbing out of his ski clothes and stripping to his thermals, Luke sits at his desk. He ignores the stack and studies his view of Vine Street below, a foot of fresh snow burying each parked car. Up the street, where a two-story apartment house has just been bulldozed, snow outlines a skeletal construction crane reaching high into the night sky. Beside it, a rectangle's been dug into the frozen earth as if for a fresh grave.

Spotlit in the streetlight, a couple shushes by on cross-country skis, cutting fresh tracks, bound for the open expanse of the park. Parked under his window, his brother's van's logo shows only the word "Adventures," the rest covered under an icy crust. The van has collected snow for weeks, immobilized since they rushed Jenn to the hospital and brought her back with his nephew in a blue bundle. Luke knows the sight of his brother's van shouldn't still jolt him. It isn't like there's going to be a resurrection. A baby in the house should be miracle enough.

But Luke doesn't believe in miracles. Easing the cat off the papers, he neatens the exams, forcing himself to dive into the responses to his essay question on the Vietnam era: *What meanings, if any, arose from so many young American deaths?*

He reaches for the pen he uses for comments, blindly feeling around the back of the top desk drawer for his green marker. Instead, his fingers graze the leather-bound journal. His summer journal, just where he'd tossed it last September. He doesn't know if he'll ever read it. Maybe he should just burn it now, like toxic evidence.

JUNE

"I hate you and your stupid happiness," his friend Emily told him, as if to inaugurate the summer.

Luke wondered if his happiness really was stupid. He was still dusty from textbook packing. A few hours before, he'd cleared out his classroom. "It's not my fault I'm a free man today, Emily."

"Today and every day of summer." She sipped the last of her wine and signaled the waiter for another. "Free as a little kid on vacation."

"I'm a teacher. It comes with the territory. But it's also the last summer of my twenties."

"And the first of your thirties. You'll be thirty before the summer's over, with no commitments, no obligations except for finishing your thesis. No children, needless to say. Instead, you're the little child of your own life. Twenty-nine and living it up in an endless state of irresponsible bliss. And a free agent in the world of romance."

"As if I have any prospects."

"Oh, you will. What are you going to do with your first week of summer? I mean, besides closing the bars on weeknights, breakfast at ten, hiking the Colorado trail, biking around canyons, and canoeing the Colorado River."

"For starters, Matt and I are just biking the trails above the river." For his older brother, a newly minted outdoor outfitter and guide, it would be a chance to scout the river route high above Horsethief Canyon, which he and Luke would then canoe in a couple weeks. "Anyway, I was thinking how the summer slips through our hands no matter how much we do or how much we enjoy it. Remember that sensation, back when we were kids, over Labor Day weekend? Like, where the hell did it go?"

"Yeah!" Emily smiled. "What the hell did I do with all that sweet time?"

"Those gorgeous blue-sky days just dissolved anyway. So, I was thinking I'd keep a journal. No big deal, just force myself every few days to record what happened, to account for every summer day."

"A body of evidence."

"Yes, for when another ideal summer existence becomes a dead body. Dropped at the schoolhouse door for an autopsy the third week of August."

After they finished their drinks, they strolled down Colfax Avenue and into a bookstore, Emily asking him, "So, how will you recognize the ideal when you have no ideals?"

Luke ignored the comment and wandered the shelves beside Emily, who had a few extra minutes before she picked up her son. They stopped at a kiosk full of notebooks and journals. Luke picked up a daily journal with a black leather-like cover and thick, lined pages. "It's expensive, but worth the splurge." He started toward the cashier. "You want one? My treat."

"No thanks," Emily said. "I got nothin' to say."

❖

In the evening of the first full day of summer, Luke sat on the back deck, tore off the journal's plastic wrap, and flipped through the empty lines. The unwritten pages already seemed gorgeous in their virginity. And mysterious. What would he be summarizing or celebrating by the last pages, what unknown adventure or new love or great book or drop-dead idea?

Luke smoothed the journal's first page and raised his favorite pen, aware of the moment's portentousness. He loved every line and curve of the date.

June 10

I'm starting this to chronicle where every summer day goes, what exactly fills these coming weeks before it all seems to vanish. After breakfast on the deck, I sat stupefied by the flood of overhead sunlight on the fruit trees beside the railing, the pear planted when Matt was born, the plum when I was. Both of them now full-grown and flourishing. I felt dizzy at the prospect of so much free time ahead, or maybe my head was just spinning from my third or fourth cup of coffee.

Before he could finish the first entry, he took a call from his brother Matt across the Rockies in Fruita, in the desert just outside Grand Junction. After confirming his arrival in Fruita the following Sunday, Luke asked, "So, everything's okay? What about those headaches?"

"About the same. But now I've got this crazy noise in my right ear. Tinnitus, Jenn says. Sometimes it's so bad I have to strain to hear what my customers are asking in the shop. Like right now, I'm moving the phone to my good ear. There. I just wonder how it's gonna be when I'm guiding groups on the river. I've got to know which canoe the voice is calling from, and right now I'm hearing so much damn static."

"Just let 'em know straight up at the gathering point, Matt. Come right out and say you might need their help."

"I don't want to sound like some half-deaf maniac right off. They've got to trust me." He changed the subject, asking if Luke had heard anything new from their parents, biologists working on a project in Ecuador. When Luke said no, Matt brought up some boyhood memory of how they tormented their parents when they teamed up on adventures. "Remember that time they freaked out when we planned to take our plastic trikes into rush-hour traffic on Colfax?"

"Just don't be the daredevil when we ride the trails on Sunday."

"We're going to start off easy. There is one hairy section where we're right over the river. A sheer drop a couple of hundred feet down the cliff. But I've got trainer wheels for you, Lukie. And a lollipop if you make it back alive."

When they finished the call, Luke watered his mother's lettuce patch before the day heated up. He didn't mind the chores at all. He was saving tons of money on rent, having given up his apartment to house-sit for his parents until they returned late in the fall. The lettuce rows were green, lush, and tufted, almost ready for the summer's first garden salad. Throw a bunch of seeds in the ground in late March, toss in some compost and fertilizer, and feast on fresh salad in June. Not a bad deal. What was wrong with cultivating happiness, then harvesting it?

Just last week at this time, Luke would've been well into his second hour class, struggling to guide his Contemporary History students as they rushed through the late 1990s, redwood tree-sit protests, airstrikes in Kosovo, and Bill Clinton's impeachment. Now he was house-sitting his own childhood home, sipping his coffee, wandering his family's back lawn barefoot. The sun poured down, nearly at its solstice apex. Phlox buds he barely had time to notice in the hectic last days of May seemed to have popped out overnight along the fences, pink and stalky, the gift of a friend's great-grandmother from a pioneer family. Their neighbors had long ago taken starts, and now the phlox's soft scent united garden to garden up and down Vine Street.

Peeking over the honeysuckle, his neighbor Judith wanted to know why his mother's lettuce was flourishing. "Over here, the slugs ate my seedlings," she said. "One morning I came out to water them, and my whole crop was gone. It was like the Bonneville Salt Flats, stark desert, not even a stub of green."

Luke savored the last of his coffee. Summer would never seem so long, so fresh, so expectant, as right now. "I haven't seen any slugs."

"I'll send some over."

❖

June 11

Damien and I went out for drinks at Aunt Pete's last night after a midnight cloudburst, the packed deck still dripping wet under cool stars. Fun to be there on a weeknight, half-price night drawing a crowd. Saw all the usual barflies for quick chats. Then this older cowpoke type, forty or so, who claimed to have a ranch in Wyoming, hit on me. He actually said I had "the body of death," whatever that means. Smirking, Damien vamoosed, like any good bar buddy, to leave me alone with the old guy. I let the cowpoke buy me a drink on the condition that I was not obliged to anything. He said he reckoned half-price cocktails don't count any more than half-obligations. Kind of witty for a cowboy. I told him I'd see him around.

He told me he'd like to see me at his summer place in the Black Hills and gave me his number.

Now in the late afternoon, big orange and purple cotton balls float in the western sky instead of the usual thunderheads. Much warmer with the sun filtering through all day, almost ready to set behind the Rockies.

I spent the morning and afternoon on all the mundane house and garden chores I put off through most of the end-of-semester madness. Went jogging at noon, found the workers putting in more flowers in new beds at Cheesman Park, masses of them from the city nurseries, making these instant garden plots ordinary backyard gardeners have to wait weeks for. Behind the pavilion, a young mother was lying beside a just-planted flower bed with her baby in her arms, as if to punctuate Denver's rebirth from the first freeze last year—when the same workers yanked out every flower and heaped the mass of dead growth into last summer's own funeral pyre.

Right now, I'm packing for my weekend with my brother on the far side of the Rockies.

❖

June 13

I had been nonplussed Matt moved even farther from Denver, but I'm really glad he chose Fruita because I would have never discovered all these trails on my own.

Matt took mercy on me for my first outing of the summer. It was hot, and I realized I needed to get into better mountain biking condition. He plans to train for a triathlon and wants me to join him for a half-marathon in the fall. We followed Mary's Loop, pretty easy, but I still had a hard time keeping up with him. At least Matt didn't insist we howl down or power up the more advanced side trails. He claimed he was ready to take it easy after his hectic late spring Sunday rush at the bike shop, but I didn't believe it. He was just being magnanimous. I've never known him to turn down a chance to kill himself up the hardest trail and spree down the steepest return.

But it was Matt who actually took a spill on one sandy section. At first I thought he was faking it, but he fell hard and bruised his ribs.

Man, I was glad it was him and not me, the family klutz. After that, he slowed down for a much more mellow ride. Matt didn't even mind when we stopped at several lookouts above the river. I think he enjoyed showing off his mind-blowing new backyard to his city-dwelling little brother. In the evening light, filtered through the junipers and mountain mahogany, the Colorado River glimmered far below, all orange and lavender, reflecting the desert sky. I just couldn't get enough of it, and Matt more than tolerated my gawking.

The last overlook put us above a cottonwood delta in Horsethief Canyon where Matt began to preview our upcoming canoe trip. He wanted me to help scout the river route before his first guided tour in July, because he claimed he'd already fallen in love with the canyon and needed a more objective eye. "Soak it in, Lukie. I'm still bedazzled by it all myself."

Sometimes, don't tell anybody, I'm still bedazzled by my big brother.

❖

On the deck of Matt's condo that night, the brothers sipped cold beers and checked their devices for any new messages from Ecuador. "Nothing," Luke said. "Guess they still haven't gotten near to any settlement that has Wi-Fi."

Matt made a face at his smartphone. "We're cyber-orphans."

Their parents were consulting biologists for an Amazonian Headwaters Society bio-blitz—"counting buds and bugs in trees"—leading teams of local and international volunteers to catalogue endangered species in an ecological preserve. Near where Ecuador met Colombia and Peru, with the borders hardly more than abstractions, they were deep in a roadless rainforest, accessible only by motorboats, then by canoe in its most remote reaches. Their comprehensive identification of rare plants and the insects in tangled canopies was meant to document the preserve's hyperintense variety of species per acre, including unique healing compounds. The Ecuadorian government had already sold leases to oil companies within the preserve. The bio-blitz had to be completed in two months, ahead of a planned onslaught of roads and housing for oil company exploration.

"What are you doing, dude?" Luke asked, noticing Matt held his beer glass at such an angle it was about to spill.

"Jeez," Matt said, righting it. "This sore rib has got me all cattywampus."

Just home from waiting tables, his girlfriend Jenn entered the deck with a beer of her own. "You've been tipping your glass like that for the last couple weeks, baby, about when you started getting those headaches." She propped herself against the railing. "Be careful."

"Maybe the distraction of my ear ringing's throwing me off balance," Matt said, shrugging. He finished his beer, then stood to perform a routine about his recent onset of tinnitus, which he mostly noticed when things quieted down in the evenings.

"I really don't mind it," he said, then raised the right side of his head in a parody, a spastic upward reach. "It has its own weird music, like shaking one of those broken old-fashioned light bulbs when we were kids. A kind of uplifting rattle," he claimed, raising his head even higher and pulling his whole body upward, as if toward that rattling music, in a clumsy ballet. "I'm just glad it's only in one ear."

"Me too," Jenn laughed, "or we'd have to watch your rattle dance twice."

Matt smiled and headed for bed, excusing himself. "Sorry for wimping out, but I've got to open the shop early tomorrow."

Luke stayed up, still alert from the evening ride. After Jenn took Matt's deck chair, he asked her about the headaches.

"He claims they're nothing, but keeps popping ibuprofen. Which usually makes him feel fine again, so it can't be too serious, right?" At Luke's prodding, she described her excitement over her summer acting class at the state college, and how her teacher encouraged her to audition for a commercial being filmed in Grand Junction. "Things are going so well,

Luke, especially Matt's business. On top of his winter gig on ski patrol here at Powderhorn."

Luke hadn't seen his brother since they'd skied free in mid-April at A-Basin courtesy of Matt's buddyhood with other ski bums at the ticket office. Watching Matt fly straight down the expert slope, fearless, Luke struggled behind him, traversing mogul to mogul just to get down alive. After their last ski, Matt spent the spring opening his new bike shop in Fruita. "This is the longest I've ever gone without seeing my brother."

"Six weeks? God, I can go a year without seeing my older sister," Jenn said. "And my folks drive me even more nuts. They're even more redneck than me, Luke. You guys, and your folks, seem so close. So educated. You have such a great family."

"We won't be good enough for you when you're a star."

"Yeah, right," Jenn said, abashed. "Did he tell you, Luke? We actually might get married."

He raised his glass and smiled. "Here's to that!"

"It won't be real soon, but we're talking that way."

"It's great to see you both doing so well." Luke gestured around the deck and the dark horizon of the Book Cliffs under a star-crowded sky. "This condo's the best place he's ever lived."

"I had doubts about moving in with him when he found this place last winter. I've done this rodeo before with outdoorsy guys. I can't sign up for the transient life again, moving on over to the next mountain when the scene gets stale. But Matt really seems to have settled down."

"Yeah, he's really found his place, his niche. Plus, the love of a good woman."

Jenn laughed, clinking his beer. "I'm not sure how good I am."

❖

June 15

I luxuriated with my coffee on the condo deck while Matt and Jenn rushed around Monday morning, he to open the shop and she to the first summer session class of her theatre program. I tried not to show how lucky I felt, in no hurry after they left, soaking in the warm morning air and blissing out on coffee, then making another summer's attempt to get through *Walden*. After suffering through twenty pages, I gave up and rode my mountain bike downtown to Matt's shop. I wanted his advice on riding the Book Cliffs trails south of town. I could tell he was frustrated by a customer complaint about a faulty derailleur, so I didn't hang around.

It's so cool the way the town's wide streets become country lanes, straight lines on the flat valley floor through ranches and little farms, the cliffs overhead looming larger. Before long, I was whoop-hollering down a roller coaster–like trail that skirted the very top of a ridge—steep drop-offs on both sides, but a fun, unthreatening descent, perfect. Though it would've been an even bigger whoop with Matt, especially now that he knows every cutoff and side route, it was about as much fun as a rider can have by himself.

❖

Back in Denver, Luke reported to Emily the latest about Matt. Luke might serve all right as her lifelong best friend, but she claimed Matt as her honorary big brother. After dinner, while Emily's son Marco watched sitcoms in the family room, Luke and Emily sat on her back patio. She absorbed the news about Matt's hearing loss. "Thirty-one just seems so young to develop that."

"Yeah," Luke said. "Maybe it's all just interference from the tinnitus, not any incipient deafness."

"Still, I wonder what it means."

"Why wonder? It probably doesn't mean anything."

"Matt's so health conscious and fit," Emily said. "Did he listen to a lot of loud music when he was younger?"

"How Catholic of you to ask. As if some sin or bad habit has brought this on. Rocking out at heavy metal concerts. Stoned on jam bands at Red Rocks. Bad, bad Matt!"

"I'm not blaming him," Emily said. "I'm just curious how hearing loss happens in such a young, healthy guy."

"Random stuff happens, right?"

"Like I don't know that, Luke?"

"Sorry. I was thinking more about health crises."

"You've got a lot of thinking to do, Luke. You've been so untouched by the really bad random stuff. You don't get it, living your perfect life."

Maybe that was true, Luke thought. Emily's tragedy had been so early and so vast that he knew it was time to listen, not say anything. Still, she did lord it over him, teasing him as the untested innocent whenever she could. Luke stared down at the golden beer, which seemed to capture the last of the late June sunlight, and he shrugged. "You could've kept teaching."

Emily leaned back. "You're right." She suppressed a sigh. "I could have."

He wished he hadn't said that. They'd made a pact to go into teaching together when they were still sophomores at Denver's East High. But Emily, widowed after teaching for just two years, quit to make more income to raise her son and help her mother with expenses.

Luke stared into Emily's backyard, a cramped swath of patchy lawn surrounding an enormous linden tree. After her husband was killed in an oil depot explosion outside Kabul, their son just four, she'd moved back to her childhood home, which had been Luke's second childhood home, too. "I'm sorry, Em. I feel like such a prick for saying that."

"You're not a prick. You're just a lucky son of a bitch, and I'm jealous."

"But you have God, and I'm just living an empty existence. I do try to be virtuous, sometimes, for the hell of it. To live well, then die pointlessly."

"You should have never taken that philosophy course. You weren't ready for it when you were a freshman, and it ruined you."

"I promote the virtuous life," Luke said, "and I'm ruined?"

"If it's pointless. If there's no cosmic justice, we're stuck in a dung hole."

"Creepy. Your conclusion, not mine."

She pointed to the first stars. "It's like saying the firmament's not really beautiful, it's just random gaseous burning blots."

"But that's what stars are."

"Did I tell you I'm getting baptized this Sunday?"

"No! Aren't you going to invite me?"

"Sure. Anyone can come. Even creepy existentialists. The priest was gravely ill during Easter vigil, so the parish is holding the adult baptisms late, and also celebrating his return to health."

Emily was born to agnostic parents, but had gone to Catholic catechism with Luke and Matt most Saturdays when they were kids. She'd drifted around Catholicism for years ever since, attending Mass with Luke's mother long after the brothers stopped going. So Emily had flirted with the Holy Spirit from an early age. When Emily met Carlos during her senior year of high school, his devout Catholic family just pushed her closer to Catholicism. Gradually, she'd become attached to her mother-in-law's parish in southwest Denver, attending Mass there and taking Become-a-Catholic classes afterward.

Emily's prior-to-wedlock pregnancy right after high school graduation complicated things but deepened her devotion to the church. Still, she'd honored her old teaching plan with Luke even while raising her baby mostly alone while Carlos was deployed to Afghanistan. With massive help from her mother, Gail, Emily joined Luke to become a certified teacher as soon as they graduated from Metropolitan State.

Luke, who had spent years shaking off all childhood indoctrinations of the church, did not really approve of Emily's Catholicism but understood his approbation was irrelevant. "I'll stop by after Mass."

"That would be very sweet."

"I feel obliged to see you duck under the holy water, drowning the Emily I've known and loved all these years."

"What will I become? A babbling Catholic automaton?"

"You said it, not me."

Emily reached for Luke's hand and clasped his fingers, raising her gaze to the stars.

❖

June 17

After pizza last night with Emily and her family and after-dinner dumbbell philosophizing on the patio, I stopped by Aunt Pete's again and ran into that Wyoming cowboy on the deck. Turns out he's staying here in Denver for some family business and wants to take me out to dinner. "Even some vegan health food place if that's what suits you," he kindly put in. I noticed for the first time how handsome he was, especially for a doddering forty-year-old.

All I said was, "Sorry, I'm not a vegan. Vegetarian, yes. Why don't you buy me that drink instead? Remember, no obligations, though."

"Obliging can be fun," he said, heading toward the bar to get our drinks.

Don't really know why I strung the cowpoke along, but I agreed on dinner by the time we finished our cocktails. There's something too sincere and ardent about him that throws me off.

❖

The cowboy ended up choosing the restaurant, an odd family-run Indian place tucked behind a storefront shared by a pot apothecary and a heavy equipment outfit on a semi-industrial stretch of Walnut Street. Luke and Jeff were the only customers at dinner, but the food was pretty good and there were lots of veggie options.

Jeff asked him about his summer studies.

"Okay," Luke said, "but remember you started it. I've got to give myself a crash course on ethical philosophers and their impact on historical events. And I love philosophy, but I mostly studied classical stuff, Plato and Aristotle, then a survey of ethics and metaphysics when I was a freshman." Jeff's eyes hadn't yet glazed over, so he asked if he knew much about Leo Strauss and other political philosophers.

"You're asking me to remember my own undergraduate philosophy survey course, and I'm at least ten years older than you are. I recall reading about Leo Strauss, but I don't know much except he was controversial, right?" Jeff said. "Too pragmatic, I think, an apologist for right-wing dictators, but then he was too atheistic for the conservatives."

Luke hoped he hid how bowled over he was. "Whew. I haven't been able to discuss philosophy with anybody in my history master's program—they think it's either too pretentious or too beside the point." Luke loved Jeff's response. He almost never got to go beyond name-dropping and bullshitting into actual wrangling with ethics and metaphysics. Emily barely tolerated the subject or tried to direct any discussion of philosophy into some Jesuit-God-almighty side channel.

"I wanted to major in philosophy at Colorado State," Jeff said, "but my parents insisted on something more practical for the family business, like, you know, animal husbandry."

❖

June 18

I wasn't even home from the Indian place when a message popped up from the Wyoming cowboy with another, more specific invitation to his family camp over the South Dakota border in the Black Hills. He'd be back up there soon and had the place all to himself. To both of us, if I wanted to join him. I couldn't think why not and agreed to take the drive at the end of the week.

So, that's where the next phase of my summer adventure's taking me. I've always wanted to check out the contours of the Black Hills. And cowboys.

❖

Luke expected barely to endure Emily's baptism, showing up out of loyalty.

She and a few other adult converts were dressed in simple white robes over their street clothes, waiting in the front pew as Mass ended. Luke slipped into the back pew in the little old church as the little old priest, crouched and shaky, led a benediction.

He'd never been anywhere near this parish, which Emily had chosen to keep connected with her husband's family. Her blond hair and blue eyes made her exotic among the dark hair and brown eyes of most of the congregation, many of whom, Emily had said, spoke Spanish.

Luke scanned the plain stone walls with their spare, crude paintings of each Station of the Cross, and the confessional behind a green velveteen curtain, appreciating the almost Protestant austerity when he spotted Emily's mother. Gail sat just behind the converts in the second row beside her grandson and his other grandmother. She turned around to catch Luke's eyes, then she smiled and kind of shrugged, as if to mime her confusion over Emily's conversion.

It must be odd for non-religious people like Gail to endure the supernatural rituals of Catholicism, especially to surrender her daughter to them. Since leaving the Church, Luke himself always felt almost paralyzed by Mass, at home in the liturgy with memorized incantations from deep in his childhood but repulsed by the shameless magic thinking.

The congregation, though, grabbed his affection: the pressed shirts and blouses, the dark, slicked-back hair of the little boys and the sculpted sports clips of their older brothers, the jangling earrings and careful makeup of the pretty moms and daughters. All the formality relaxed now that Mass was over. A boisterous energy shot through the pews, sweet release and companionability coming to life in that brief intermission before the baptisms began, loud whispers of family gossip. Then all was hushed by the first convert's call to the baptismal font, the feeble old priest now twinkly eyed as he spoke the magic words and sprinkled the magic water. Next was Emily herself, her shapely, strong body seeming to wiggle as it rebelled against the plain white robe. Still, she bowed her head in submission, her long golden locks lush and cascading.

Luke gulped back surprise at his tears, swiping them quickly. It made no sense, being so moved by the sacrament, which he thought was another grand mistake of Emily's—right up there with getting pregnant just out of high school—her joining this ancient and deeply fucked-up outfit. The tears were vestiges, he thought, calming down, of his indoctrination at such a young age, sentiments still banishing rational thought. A semi-automatic slip into faith from the healthier nothingness of existence.

On the front steps afterward, he felt like the surrogate husband, a stand-in as Gail took his arm and cooed soothing words about how pleased she was that he decided to attend. "I know you're no more of a believer than I am, Luke," she confided, stage-whispering, "but it's so good of you to be here. It means the world to Emily."

"That's the reason I'm here, too," Luke said, pulling Gail into a hug and kissing her on the cheek. "Because Emily means the world to me."

"Sometimes I wish..." she said, then stopped. "I won't say it. There's nothing to say, because you're perfect the way you are, Luke. A perfect friend to Em. I love you, kid."

While Emily was laughing and chatting with her mother-in-law, her son Marco slipped from her side and, in a kind of running dance, sidestepped down the steps to stand at Luke's. He would soon be twelve, shooting up higher every time Luke saw him. A month ago, his eyes had been at Luke's chin, and now, in his dress shoes, he seemed almost eye-to-nose with his agnostic godfather. Elongating like taffy, his basic mass stayed the same but stretched, impossibly skinny. Emily said he literally had growing pains, crying out at the jabs of bone aches.

"Hey Luke," Marco said, his voice suddenly deeper, "it must be weird for you to show up at church, huh?"

"Pretty weird, yeah," Luke said, turning down his voice, hoping Marco would follow suit. "But I've been making my peace with the Church as time goes on."

"That's why I was asking. Why show up in a church that hates fags?"

"Marco!" Gail gasped. "Don't talk to Luke that way. And don't use that word, it's ugly."

"That word isn't cool, Marco." Luke tried to take it calmly. "And I wouldn't say the Catholic hierarchy hates gays. But you're right that they don't really accept us as equals."

"Maybe there's stuff about gays that's disgusting to, like, God."

Emily, who had started to join the group but held back on an upper step during the exchange with Marco, now stepped down, simultaneously giving Luke's arm a quick caress and seizing Marco's as she led him away, down to street level. Face-to-face, she caught Marcos's gaze, which she held in stern steadiness as she spoke with determination some reprimand Luke couldn't hear. When Marco turned away, abrupt and angry, to sulk beside an urn full of fledgling geraniums beside the staircase, Emily shook her head for Luke's benefit as she made her way up the steps.

"Don't be too rough on him," Luke muttered to her, trying out a smile. He'd never told Marco he was gay, but he must've heard about it or figured it out on his own. Luke had always felt paternal toward him, and in an unspoken way had co-fathered him with Matt ever since Carlos was killed. When Marco started middle school, Luke had made a point of speaking to him more frankly and encouraging him to do the same in return. Was this what came of that, now, enduring Marco's confusion as well as his insolence?

"Oh, I'm gonna be rough enough," Emily said, beside Luke now. "I don't want him to develop any more of those bigoted attitudes."

"Who knows, though?" Luke said. "God may very well find me disgusting."

❖

Luke spent the days before his trip to the Black Hills in a jumble of disconnected activity. He couldn't tell one of these summer days from another, the perfect warm stillness of the sunny mornings, the sharp, hot early afternoons followed by building clouds, wind, thunder, and gutter-washing downpours, then calm, cool, starry nights.

He swam laps at the rec center, then dried off in the noon

sun, hoping to impress the cowboy with his tan. Then he worked out in the weight room, hoping to impress the cowboy with his pecs and biceps. But that could only happen, he thought, if the cowboy was easily impressed.

He picked apart a stubborn weed patch occupying a corner of the vegetable garden until afternoon rains turned his uprooted progress into muddy maelstroms. Sheltered in his office, he began moving paper around or surfing websites for the summer's academic project, his thesis for a master's in American history.

Close to midnight, he stopped by Aunt Pete's in hopes of sharing a drink with a bar buddy, defining "buddy" very loosely, then going home well before closing time.

The cowboy texted provocative updates, claiming to be taking lessons in vegetarian cooking and washing his sheets for the first time in the season; then he emailed extensive directions to the summer place with many cautionary sub-instructions about what to do after taking the wrong turn after the wrong junction and taking the wrong way at obscure T-intersections on Black Hills back roads.

Matt wanted to nail down dates for their canoe trip and texted to invite Luke back to Fruita to explore the single-track trail network in the forested slopes of Glade Park.

Emily wanted to know if he would ever forgive Marco for his outburst on the church steps.

Luke had already forgotten about Marco's indiscreet words. He felt ever warmer toward both Emily and his brother. He was looking forward to another Fruita trip, his head too full of fantasies about cowboy time in the Black Hills for anything but magnanimity.

❖

June 20

It was five hours to the Black Hills, then at least another half hour just wandering the back roads trying to follow Jeff the Cowboy's instructions. The way north, I kept thinking about how reckless spending a weekend with a near stranger was. After I left the numbered roads, the route became too remote for any help from GPS. Following Jeff's intricate instructions on ever twistier nameless lanes where no one can hear you yell for your life, I had plenty of time to wonder about whether the cowboy was really a mass murderer luring guys to his rusty trailer in the deep woods. His name is even Jeffrey, spelled like Dahmer's.

But Jeffrey just brought me a beer and then left me in peace on his deck to write this, overlooking a little lake surrounded by pines. His family's summer place is hardly a camp—it's a full-size, if compact, house complete with wood shingle siding and four-pane windows. Rustic French doors lead out to this deck, which wraps around two sides of the place and leads into a big living room with knotty pine paneling straight out of some old-time rumpus room where the mounted heads of a magnificent elk, a ferocious open-mawed bear, a startled buck, and a placid mountain goat stare down from three walls. Jeffrey must have caught my silent consternation, because he explained that the mounted heads were relics from long-gone family members. Judging by this swanky cabin held for generations and his big black Beamer 4x4, my cowboy ain't exactly no poor ranch hand.

His intentions may be honorable since I have my own guest room. We'll see how that works out. His good manners might be all for misdirection. He could still be a cannibal.

❖

While Luke was changing after his shower, Jeff knocked on the guest room door and poked in. "Dang, you're almost decent, kid. Bad timing."

Luke pulled his T-shirt over his jeans. "I promise to show you a little ankle if you stop calling me kid."

"That can be arranged, sir."

Luke was struck by Jeffrey's big green-gray eyes. The way the lids were kind of lazy and heavy, usually at half mast as if to show off his thick lashes. "My ankles are particularly spectacular."

"Like so much of you, I'll bet."

"Don't waste a wager. I tend toward scrawny compared to the buffed gods I'm sure you're used to luring here."

"Yeah, but I'm so weary of buffed gods." He sat on the bed while Luke found clean socks in his suitcase. "I'm interested in exploring scrawny."

"Not to change the subject, but I couldn't open that closet. Is it stuck or locked?"

"Both. We don't use it."

"We?"

"The family. A rotating cast of parents, brothers, and cousins all have a claim, and somebody has a claim on that closet. And the key. I was lucky to get the place for a June weekend. What'd you want the closet for, anyway?"

"I thought I'd hide my suitcase in there. Speaking

of closets, does your family know you've arranged male companionship as part of your rotating claim?"

"More or less. I tend not to advertise my companions, though. Family gossip is intense, whether gay or straight."

Luke sat on the bed beside him. "Must be lonely out here."

"Not this weekend." Jeffrey's kiss was urgent, pressing and prolonged, but his lips were soft. He pulled off Luke's T-shirt with expert dispatch and started undoing his belt, saying, "I hope you don't mind stripping off what you just put on."

"It's no trouble, believe me," Luke said, raising his legs to help Jeffrey pull off his jeans.

❖

June 22

Longest day of the year, and I'm feeling decadent, elongating my farewell to the Black Hills with another cup of coffee here on the deck. I'm not used to being pampered, least of all out here in the hills, where the strong scent of the sun on the pines is getting obliterated by the bacon Jeff's frying up for brunch—pig for him, veggie strips for me.

He took me on the Black Hills grand tour yesterday, the tourist trifecta of Crazy Horse monument, Mount Rushmore, and Deadwood. Cool to finally see the highlights, but I loved everything in between the best, the miles of rolling pine hills, lakes and streams, an undulating plateau of forest, mellow and nestled, nothing like the relentless inclines and ravines of Colorado's high country. Jeff really is pretty keen for philosophy and history, which meant I got to try out my scattered thesis ideas on him. To my flabbergasted exhaustion, we couldn't stop yakking about ethical philosophers on the long stretches between sites. We stopped for late lunch at a little family café unchanged since the 1940s. The veggie option? Grilled cheese on white bread. Now, that's decadence.

I'm weak-kneed from lovemaking. Jeff's is this kaleidoscopic surging of aggressive and gentle. Sweet Baby Jesus, he's pretty spunky for an old dude of forty. The first official day of summer could not be more inviting. Like, right now. I'm being called to sample the fake bacon.

❖

After brunch, Jeff had to go east to Rapid City for a family business thing, but Luke wanted to drive back to Denver via the west route out of the hills to Livingston, Wyoming, where Jeff's ranch spread over high grasslands. "If you insist," Jeff told him, "but I don't think you're going to find acres of grazing cattle very compelling."

"Maybe you'll find this compelling." Luke passed him an old issue of *Harper's*. He'd finally finished an article that compared the ethics of Leo Strauss, the conservative philosopher they'd discussed at the Indian place, and Peter Singer, whose contrasting premises seemed seminal to understanding the left-right split in contemporary politics from abortion to animal rights, and whose names continued to come up in their halting, hey-we're-just-half-educated-dudes-trying-to-discuss-philosophy-in-South-Dakota-without-getting-too-deep-in-our-own-bullshit.

Jeff accepted the magazine, regarding the cover with a

smile. "Gee, I always wanted to dive into Singer vs. Strauss."
Then he yanked off the mailing label, studied it, and carefully
folded it and slipped it in his shirt pocket. "If you don't mind,
Mr. Devlin. Now, I've got your address."

"It's obsolete, Mr. Douglas. I had to give up that apartment.
Now I'm house-sitting for my parents until they get back from
Ecuador in the fall." He explained his folks' species inventory
project in remote tributaries of the Amazon.

Jeff locked up the cabin and led Luke to his car. "Species
inventory?"

"Mom counts blossoms, and Dad identifies butterflies."

❖

Driving out of the Black Hills, Luke was tempted to break
his free agency rule. After some lousy luck with boyfriends,
near-boyfriends, and never-were-boyfriends throughout his
twenties, he was ready to declare a truce with coupling and
commitment here at the end of an entire decade of trying to
establish them. The rule was to stop dreaming about a long-
term relationship, to admit that it wasn't possible in his corner
of the universe. Serial couplings were his fate.

Now he wondered if this free agency in love was really
self-deceit, a cover to hide future disappointments. After his
weekend with Jeff, Luke felt an opposing temptation to junk
the rule and start dreaming of going steady again.

He had to admit, Jeffrey Douglas was a great guy,
intelligent and funny, and it didn't hurt that he was good-
looking, well-built, sexy, and heir to a ranching fortune. That
last quality made Luke feel as if his life had wondered into a
nineteenth-century novel about marriage choices and fortunes,
a distant world from his own, where fortunes were nonexistent.

His choices were often reduced to finding someone interested in clothing brands and TV celebrities or the much smaller numbers of those curious about the great world and willing to plunge into it together.

As the pines began to thin and the hills flattened, the backcountry route met US 85, and Luke realized he had crossed out of South Dakota back into Wyoming's wide-open high plains. Under a blue sky dappled by thin, stretched clouds, juniper and yellow rabbitbrush lined the highway. Snow fences started to line the empty roadside, then behind them an occasional steer soon joined another, until the whole plain was dotted with cattle. This fit Jeff's description of the panorama Luke expected, a wide vista of grazing, peaceable beasts roaming to far horizons.

In a few miles, the highway crested a low ridge and curved into a shallow valley. A creek produced a line of cottonwoods and tangles of evergreen brush. On the other side of the highway bridge, a gravel road led west along the valley's shapely flatlands, bordered by low ridges. Luke swerved onto the gravel road and followed it to a distant group of buildings under a copse of cottonwoods. In the shelter of the valley, the trees swayed gently, casting shifting shadows.

Luke slowed to study the buildings. They clustered like a village in the creek's wide bend. A large modern house dominated the site, clad in varnished logs. Stone steps led to where enormous, sinuous log posts formed an arched roof. Two little boys tossed a plastic football on a plush stretch of lawn inside a paved circular drive that lassoed the whole complex.

It was all so tidy and perfectly maintained it seemed like an advertisement for itself. An embossed sign hung from the polished post-and-beam gate: Thunder Creek Family Ranch, Homesteaded 1889.

Luke drove on, enjoying the expanse where the gravel road rose to the dry ridge, punctuated by cattle munching on the slope.

Nothing in the valley prepared him for the scene on the other side of the ridge. He pulled over at the summit to survey it. Every inch of the flattest land was cut into hundreds of small metal-fenced stalls, each confining a steer unable to move more than a few inches fore or aft. The land under the stalls was mucky with cattle shit, a continuous dark stain from the banks of the creek to the farthest ridge. A steady breeze pushed the stench inside Luke's car.

Enormous metal-roofed industrial buildings framed the acres of stalls, each arrayed with long, complicated ramps. A holding pond, bubbling with more manure and saturated earth, sealed off the sludge from the creek. Across it, structures like extra-large pet transporters lined the other side of the valley, like tombstones in an overcrowded graveyard.

As Luke squinted to figure out the purpose of the tombstone-like structures, he was startled by a tapping on his driver's side window, the handle of a flashlight tapping the glass. Now Luke spotted the pickup parked twenty yards down the slope. A husky man in a light flannel shirt and a red cap signaled for him to lower his window. "Gotta ask what you're doing here. This is private land."

"Sorry." Letting in the breeze, Luke gagged a bit on the wafting stench. "I thought it was a public road."

"It's not. You taking any pictures?"

"No, sir. I was just touring the ranch."

"Gotta ask if you're a reporter or activist."

Luke tried to smile. "Nope. I'm a history teacher."

"Spotted your Colorado plates. You know we gotta enforce Wyoming's Data Trespassing Bill. Means I confiscate any pictures you're taking of the operations."

"My phone and my camera are in my pack. I haven't used them." Luke gestured toward the back seat, where he'd tossed his day pack. "I was just visiting the Black Hills with Jeffrey Douglas and stopped here to see his family's ranch."

"Oh. You a friend of Jeff's?" The man in the red cap burst into a smile and lowered the bludgeon-like flashlight. Almost sheepish, he explained that their operations were constantly under threat from snoopers, spies from the conglomerates that ran multiple ranches statewide. He shook Luke's hand through the open window and apologized. "Any friend of Jeff's is welcome to have a look around. Any time. But I gotta do my job, see?"

Luke said he understood and returned a wave in farewell. But, scanning the stinking feedlot and the ramped factory buildings, he realized he had no claim on understanding. He strained to comprehend why a feedlot would be in the middle of such a windy rapture of open pasture.

❖

June 24

I got home late yesterday and today got caught up on all the usual house management tasks and errands, plus dealing with billing deadlines for the parents' annual city tax and insurance payments. Weeded junk mail stacks for hidden non-junk, then actually weeded the veg and flower beds, each of which could be a full-time job. Not to mention cleaning the cat's litter box. Harvested a nice slug-free bag of lettuce for Judith, who repaid me by asking me to get out the high ladder and unblock one of her downspouts. Later she brought over a prepared salad with feta and artichokes and told me I was looking skinnier and skinnier since my "mommy fled to the Amazon." I told her I've gained five pounds, which I blame on too many sociable beers, then I ran six miles at twilight to help melt off the blubber. Moved thesis notes around on my desk, thinking of Peter Singer, utilitarianism and animal rights, trying to understand how ethical philosophy intersects with history in all of its deliberation and randomness.

Jeff messaged me about connecting when he's in Denver on business next week. Can't wait to ask him about his ranch's operations. Damien messaged me in hopes of going for drinks at Aunt Pete's, but I'm not in the mood. It's usually dead on Tuesdays anyway, so I promised him I'd join him on half-price night Thursday. Email from Mom and Dad, who want to set up a video call tomorrow while they're in Tena for supplies.

Not every summer day is actually worth all this ink.

❖

Luke propped up his parents' old cat so they could see him on the computer's video chat. After oohing and ahhing, his mother wondered if the screen was making Toonces look fat. "Are you feeding him too much, honey?"

"He's a cat, Mom. He's always diving face-first into his food."

"Maybe try rationing a little bit?"

Luke's father leaned in and squeezed onscreen to ask about blistering paint in the soffits, basement leaks, and his other minor but persistent drainage worries.

"You guys are in the middle of the Amazon, on one of the most important research projects in biological history, and all you can do is obsess about a geriatric cat and gutters on an old house on Vine Street in Denver?"

"We're not in the middle of the Amazon, Lukie," his father said. "Our tributary is actually on the western edges of the watershed."

"And Tena is actually quite close to the Andes," his mother put in. "It feels so civilized. Electricity, hot showers, and my son's face on this screen."

Luke rushed to squeeze in the news of Matt's engagement. His mother started clapping, her face lost in a video blur of joyous abandon. His father just smiled. "You'll have your mother fantasizing about grandchildren for the rest of our project."

"Hell yes I will!" his mother managed to say, laughing. "I've been so jealous of Gail having Marco all these years."

When they pressed him for details, Luke realized he'd jumped the gun in his excitement to share the news, because he didn't really have any good details. "They're pretty vague about wedding plans. They'll probably wait until you guys get back to the States."

Finally, his father hinted they didn't have much longer on the computer. "It's so great to connect, son. We miss the hell out of you."

"Me too, you guys!"

Luke's last words might not have been heard when the video chat shut off. His parents might have jinxed it by praising "electricity" and "connection" which were shaky even in the semi-civilized precincts of Tena, the frontier capital of Ecuador's Amazonian province.

❖

June 25

Jeff popped up on the screen only a few minutes after I lost contact with Drs. Ted and Kathy Devlin in Tena. I apologized in advance that I might switch back to them if their connection was restored, but Jeff just wanted me to know he was coming to Denver on Sunday for business and could I reserve some time Sunday evening? I didn't even pretend to check my calendar. I didn't bother to hesitate. I just said sure and even told him he looked rather dashing on video chat, and wondered why I always looked such a dork. He agreed I did. "But a very cute dork."

I never did reconnect live with Mom and Dad. They sent an email later cc'ing Matt, explaining how disappointed they were not to connect/chat at all with him before the power went out. Now, they wrote, they were hurrying to send the message that they were already packing for the truck/boat/canoe odyssey back down to their research camp on the River Napo. And, oh yeah, they wanted me to check the soffits for leaks. And to be sure to put Toonces on a diet.

❖

June 26

Matt laughed when I told him about Dad and the soffits and Mom and the fat cat. "That's the way Ted'n'Kathy tell us they love us, little brother," he said, and I could almost hear his smile. I knew it was followed by that wistful look he gets when he thinks of our parents so far away, counting skippers' wings and uncategorized jungle flowers. Though it was just a smartphone call, no screenshots, I could plainly visualize what Matt saw chatting from his condo deck at dusk, the Book Cliffs over the rooftops of the tract homes to the north, the rough sandstone tops of the escarpment catching the last of the sunlight in a bronze blaze while the heat furnace of the valley floor cooled into evening.

We firmed up the dates next week when we'll take our practice canoe run on the Colorado River to scout camping spots for his first guided tour weekend in mid-July for a Telluride family celebrating their mother's birthday, the inauguration of Horsethief Adventures. He needs to test his canoes, equipment, and supplies, and since he knows the river's course by heart and I'm a virgin in Horsethief and Ruby Canyons, he wants to monitor my reactions and anticipate my questions.

He wants to test out his hearing on the river itself, sure it'll be fine despite the tinnitus. Matt's excited about the launch of his own river and bike tour company geared to small groups and families, and still seems incredulous he has paying clients lined up for July and August. "You're lucky, Luke! I wish I could paddle Ruby and Horsethief Canyons for the first time. It's gonna blow your mind."

Jenn came on the line to tell me her own big career breakthrough. She got the gig! She'll be the spokeswoman for a series of commercials for clean energy, playing a young geologist/environmentalist, all of them filmed around Grand Junction, the Mesa, and the Monument.

Damien's coming through the door. It's time, he says, to score cheap drinks and cheaper men at Aunt Pete's.

❖

June 27

Biked to Congress Park pool for a swim, early enough to jog to and around Cheesman Park in the noon heat before diving into the merciful water. I think I'm getting back in summer shape and may avoid being as bloated as Toonces after all. I even got whistled by two leering guys in an open Jeep where the jogging path crosses Ninth Avenue. After pool laps and drying off in the sunshine, sudden dark thunderclouds followed me home, where the afternoon rain helped me stay fixed to my desk long enough to concentrate on my thesis.

I'm narrowing down opposing ethical views—Singer's compassionate utilitarianism and Strauss's free-market pragmatism—to apply to the historic implications of the Summitville Mine disaster, complicated claims stretching back to Colorado's settlement culminating in cyanide spills in 1990 that contaminated the Alamosa River watershed.

It felt good to write it all down in a kind of free association that actually started at Aunt Pete's last night. The minute I got to the insanely packed patio, with Damien at my side almost jumping out of his skin with excitement, I realized I didn't want to be jostled and poked, stuck in a barely moving mass of men fueled by too much vodka and beer. I missed

Jeff's company. Right now, nobody else interested me, and nobody else is interested in discussing Singer and Strauss. At Aunt Pete's, I kept company with my thoughts and found a corner, nursing a cocktail and pondering the ethical complications of cyanide releases into the Alamosa River.

Damien slithered between the high tables with another guy in tow, tall, slender, about my age, whom Damien deposited at my side while he returned to the bar for more drinks, saying this guy's got important news about "your cowboy."

The guy was nice enough, except for how his smiles kept snarking into slight smirks. "Damien says you spent a weekend with the cowboy. Just be careful. It's not just his cattle that are full of bullshit."

When I moved closer to hear him better and ask what he meant, another guy appeared at his side to tug him away. Apparently, he was perpetually in tow or tug, and he disappeared into the mass of rowdy men. I never had a chance to find out more.

❖

"I can't make you talk to me, Marco," Luke said. "But I sure miss our conversations."

"That's too bad, because I'm not talking to you."

Emily had sent Marco up to his room after he refused to eat the Chinese takeout—"fag food"—Luke brought over for their Friday dinner, then refused to say anything at the table. After dinner, Luke checked on Marco in his detention upstairs and carefully kept his distance, standing half in, half out of the bedroom doorway. "Maybe it's too bad for you, too, because I'm not going anywhere. Your mom is my best friend. Your grandma and my mother always been best friends, too, you know. Emily and I started kindergarten together. We took First Communion together. So you're going to have to sulk by yourself for the rest of your life."

"I'm not sulking. I just don't get why you turned gay when Matt turned out normal. I just hate how you changed."

"I didn't change. I was born this way. I never lied to you about who I was. But I was waiting until you were older before I told you the whole story."

"It doesn't matter how much older I get." Propped on his bed pillows, Marco slipped on his baseball mitt and methodically knocked his fist into the palm pocket. "I'll always hate you."

"Okay, so hate me. But why don't you apologize to your mom for your behavior at dinner and help yourself to some Chinese food?"

"I don't need to. I can sweet talk Granma into giving me some later."

"Well, I'm not giving up on you."

"Well, I'm giving up on you." Marco pounded the mitt with his fist. "So leave me alone."

Luke took the stairs slowly, as if he didn't want them to creak, as if extreme care on each step would somehow compensate for his complete failure to win Marco over. What Luke really wanted to do was walk out of the house and down the darkening street by himself to tend to the wound he felt from Marco's words and tone, this kid who'd openly admired him and begged for his company three weeks ago. This kid slapping the mitt Luke had given him for his last birthday. Damn.

Instead, Luke found Emily on the patio, staring at the night sky, tears sliding down her face. He raised her head and kissed her on the forehead. He dried her tears, swiping them off with his fingers. "I'm sorry, Em. But I never said anything."

"I know you didn't. I think he overheard some conversation Mom and I were having. This is what we get for talking about you behind your back. I'm the one who's sorry."

"He's still too young to understand this. He's probably hearing things at school."

"Or maybe he's just a little prick, Luke, have you thought of that? Maybe he just wants to hurt you and me and sit back and enjoy the damage."

"Come on. Marco and I always got along well before this."

"So, now he's showing his true colors. He's always resented me, I think, because his dad is gone, and you were a surrogate dad, and now—"

"He feels betrayed, maybe."

"I want to at least entertain the possibility that he's got an evil streak. Just like his father, who wanted to be involved in explosives, who wanted to rain down violence."

"Come on, Emily. Don't bring evil into it. There's probably no such thing, anyway. Marco's a good kid."

"You're only seeing now what I've been seeing for years. This same stubborn mean streak. He never revealed it to you because he revered you. He puts men on a pedestal."

"Straight men."

"And meanwhile, women are already his inferiors. He's shaping up to have quite a lot of his father's side of the DNA, I'm telling you, and I don't know how to prevent that."

"Man, Em, don't talk yourself into something horrible. Marco's hearing all kinds of messed-up shit in middle school. I remember hearing the same stuff and believing the fags were sick psychos. It's a phase, a pathetic boy thing."

"I hope so. But you know me, Luke. I believe in essences, remember? I think there's an essence to a person that may not derive only from their experience."

"A soul? Okay. But a soul can't be evil."

"Why the hell not?"

"Because it derives from God."

Emily sighed and reached for her water glass. She sipped and stared at the dark yard. "I love how you existentialist atheists worship your all-benevolent God. Meanwhile, evil might be genetically implanted into the son I love."

"Let's not be tempted by that. Let's give Marco some space to be a stubborn, messed-up boy, okay?" Luke reached for Emily's hand and squeezed it. "Let's just go on loving him."

❖

Luke thought nothing was quite like washing down naan bread with a smear of chutney and Kingfisher beer in the company of a Wyoming cowboy. This time in the obscure Indian place there was one other couple, plus an older South Asian man eating alone in a far corner. "This place is too good to be so empty."

"I think they do most of their business with a lunch buffet. It's cheap, and the River North hipsters line up for it. But for dinner, they really do cook to order." Jeff swiped at the remaining curry with the last of his naan. "I like being here like this, just me and you. It's our tradition."

"Two dinners out do not a tradition make, Mr. Douglas. So, what exactly brings you to Denver?"

"I usually have to deal with family business here, including serving on a cattlemen's board, at least once a month. More, if I want to seek the company of a cute guy."

"It's a long drive for cute company."

"Wyoming's a big empty place."

Luke worked up his nerve enough to explain that he'd seen the feedlot and gotten interrogated by a guard. "I just don't get it, those cattle confined to those tiny stalls in the middle of such a big empty place."

"It's normal, Luke. If you weren't a city kid, you'd know that. Most ranches do it. Cattle roam the range land most of their lives, then spend their last months getting fattened up in a feedlot."

"But they can barely move their heads from side to side, let alone turn around. It's like they're in solitary confinement."

"I know. I think about it all the time myself. But it's just the standard methodology I inherited and the standard of all the operations surrounding ours. It's a norm that seems obscene and cruel through fresh eyes like yours."

"It is cruel."

"Compared to what happens to the poor beasts next, in the slaughterhouse?"

"They still don't have to spend their last weeks in misery, Jeff," Luke said, aware that he was sounding like any given clueless city kid.

❖

June 29

Jeff's rationalizations last night sure sounded like bullshit. I wonder if that's what the slender guy in the bar was talking about. Maybe it's having grown up in a vegetarian family, but I can't figure out how people can stomach the real story of how the meat gets to their plate and into their mouths. Even if it's not exactly karma, devouring a steak has to include ingesting all the treatment of that animal, up to and including its violent slaughter. You're eating its suffering. Maybe people don't even think about it, any more than Jeff was really much fazed by his family's "standard methodology," and don't give it any more thought than I give to my leather belts and shoes, which is to buckle them up and ignore thinking about it and whether it's consistent with my own family's "standard methodology."

And my high-minded ethics certainly didn't stop me from enjoying last night and this morning with Jeff in his room at the Oxford downtown. It's so easy between us. He has that natural eroticism that helps relax me, but also has the ardor and pent-up urgency of sex, reducing us to animal groans, that takes us to such powerful climaxes. After, we roll around laughing.

We lingered in the sheets well into midmorning, then strolled into Union Station for breakfast feeling languid and privileged, taking our sweet time among the travelers and business people hustling to their next appointments. Jeff didn't have one until ten thirty, and my only appointment was to head to the pool for more mindless laps in the stinging, sharp noon heat. Then at home I checked in with my absent thesis advisor via video chat, projecting a poor imitation of a coherent history grad student.

I finished packing for the canoe trip, trying not to fantasize about living as the only vegetarian cowpoke on my husband's Wyoming cattle ranch.

❖

During the last spur of Horsethief Canyon, before the railroad began to line river right, Luke paddled with his big brother into pure, late morning bliss. It was one of those moments when life seems to embrace the one living it. An exalted grace mixed with gratitude for the sheer fact of existence. Matt had fallen silent, too, steering the canoe at the rear, with only the sound of rhythmic plashing as the river carved its route through the rugged walls. It seemed impossible for a Colorado native whose adventurous parents had taken him to so many trails, ravines, and canyons in the foothills and high country that Luke had never really ventured into these red rock deserts near the Utah border. In the family's hurry to cross the state line and reach the Canyonlands around Moab, this area had been no more than a blur on the interstate between the alpine summits of Colorado and the sandstone arches and slickrock of southern Utah. Now that Matt had moved to Fruita, so close to Colorado's western border, Luke felt he had a personal guide to a vast new playground within his home state.

"You were too young to remember, but Ted'n'Kathy went through a big canoe phase when you were still a rug rat. We only did this canyon once, though, after they fell in love with rowdier currents in Dominguez Canyon."

"I remember Dominguez! The little waterfall in that side canyon."

"Yeah, we canoed that stretch several times. Mom and Dad always said rivers were sacred, which I thought was so over the top, but now I know what they meant. Then I think they just got tired of schlepping canoes and camping equipment, including the two of us, and trying to cram all that fun into summer weekends, then face the office or lab on Monday."

"They were pretty amazing, though, about how many weekends they were willing to schlep stuff, like those overnight backpacks in Lost Creek and Indian Peaks."

"Say that again, Lukie? This damn tinnitus is driving me nuts again. Sorry. Suddenly it's starting to bug me during daylight, too."

Atop the canyon rim to the east, Luke could see the very spot where they had looked down on the Colorado River from the Kokopelli bike trail. This felt too magical for real life; to declare a plan and then find yourself paddling down the very river two weeks later as if looking back at yourself making it.

Midafternoon, just when all shade disappeared under a bloated, demon-hot sun, they reached Black Rocks, where Matt planned to set up the overnight camp. As the river narrowed and Matt shouted instructions, Luke whooped at their first and only true rapid so far. Whitecapped riffles sped them over quick crests, a fast, chewy spree just where the heavy current plunged between dark, rounded rock formations.

At the point where they turned to slip onto a beach between the rocks, Luke heard an incomprehensible yell and a loud splash and felt the weight in the back lighten while the canoe rocked, askew. Getting on his knees up front, Luke paddled forward toward the beach, listing enough to take on water before he righted the canoe with desperate, lunging dragging pulls and nosed it toward the beach. As he jumped out, grabbing the rope, he looked back at two objects in the shallow water—one of their red river bags floating in the calm cove, and Matt, wet from cap to feet, still clutching his paddle and laughing.

"Damn! In one damn half-second flash, there goes my lifetime of bragging rights. I've never capsized a canoe before, not once."

"Well, you still haven't. The canoe didn't capsize,

you did." Luke fetched the errant river bag. "What the hell happened?"

"Hell if I know. Just suddenly felt like I was rocking the wrong way, off-balance."

"Was it me?"

"No, you were just fine, Luke. It was all my doing. I'm the one steering, but I can't explain what happened." He stood up, shaking his head, steadying himself in the soft sand, and laughed again. "Damn, brother!"

"You still think the river is sacred?"

After they set up their tent on a sandy ledge overlooking the river, the brothers beat the heat with what Matt called a Black Rocks classic: floating the long, easy rapid on their backs, buoyed up by life jackets. Hooting toward the beach, they'd climb around the smooth black formation to do it over and over again. Side by side, sliding down the lip of cool liquid together, Matt honed his guide's spiel about the rocks' geology. "I love this place. It's maybe my favorite place in the universe. Out of nowhere, out of this relatively young sandstone, this one-point-five-billion-year-old metaphoric rock shows its face. Dark like the Earth before life began!"

Wrapped in the river's delicious chill, then clambering back into the searing heat, then plunging into the green-blue relief again, Luke had no trouble agreeing Black Rocks was an earthly paradise. When they finally surrendered to the onset of evening, they threw down their life jackets on the beach and reclined on them to dry in the waning sunlight.

"So, you guys twins?" They looked up to see a heavy guy in a Rockies ball cap, bearing a canned beer in an insulated holder, raising his brim in greeting.

Luke and Matt sat up, laughing. "No. If you look carefully," Luke said, "you'll see I'm younger and taller and better looking."

"Sorry, friend," Matt said to Rockies Cap, raising his hand to the side of his face, covering his mouth from Luke's view. "We trained him to say that whenever he's asked. My little brother, he's kind of special."

Rockies Cap laughed, crouching to shake hands with each of the brothers, explaining he was camping just downriver. Matt immediately began to pick his brain about his likes and dislikes about the available campsites while Luke caught the sun sinking behind the jagged canyon wall, thankful to watch it disappear.

❖

June 30

Matt's conked out in the tent already, so I'm writing this by the glow of my headlamp, propped against a rock, butt in the soft sand. Already this journal is showing summer's wear and tear, a little bent from its journey here at the bottom of my river bag. The cool river's surging by, and the stars are crazy clear.

Matt treated me as his guinea pig for dinner; not to eat guinea pig but to sample the Veggie Pasta Sublime he's testing for his clients. Jenn was supposed to be his co-chef, but she had location shooting on Grand Mesa and might not be able to partner with Matt on the canoe guiding gig at all. Who knows where her commercial stardom is going to take her next month? Old Matt didn't do too badly by himself with my help chopping veggies, but the cheese sauce is definitely too bland. Garlic, brother! After we cleaned up, we took a twilight hike a short way up Moore Canyon, but Matt stumbled on some of the rocks when it started getting darker, then fell hard, luckily onto a sandy patch. But he still smacked his side pretty badly. He's sure now the tinnitus is whacking up his balance. When I told him he should see his doctor, he said he heard there's no cure for it, that people just get used to it, and that he doesn't have a doctor, anyway. Hasn't ever been to a doctor as an adult, except once to a sports clinic for shin splints after a half-marathon.

I asked, what made him think he was an adult?

Matt's snoring now. It's 9:15 Mountain Daylight Time.

JULY

July 2

After the inferno of a July afternoon in the Grand Valley, a passing rainless thunderstorm cooled it down enough for Jenn and Matt to venture out to their deck and brave the gas grill. We did a steak for Jenn and veggie burgers for the Devlin brothers, along with roasted potatoes, peppers, and mushrooms "for the whole family" as Jenn, who was in an expansive mood, said, pouring a local Palisade Red. After the day's shoot, she'd just been given samples of the wine from the production company. "These guys have deep pockets. They spend more on our snack buffets during a shoot than I make in a week of waiting tables, first-rate stuff and top-drawer booze at the end of the shoot. All for a series of thirty-second commercials."

"Where do they get all this crazy money?" Matt asked, flipping peppers.

"I'm not sure the Clean Energy Council is what it sounds like," Jenn said. "Where would conservationists get this kind of money?"

Luke wondered if he should venture into these waters at all. But Matt soon asked Jenn what he wanted to: "So, it's like, oil and gas?"

"My lines are all about the pretty Colorado landscape and how important it is to preserve for my children. Apparently, I have a brood of toddlers, all of whom I will take for long walks in the wild as soon as they stop toddling and start walking. It's Vanessa, you know, my character. And she's 'real,' a 'conservation energy geologist.' She loves nature but understands that we need energy, too."

"We do, but from fracking?"

"I just read the lines, Matt. I ride up to the Grand Mesa in a Cadillac SUV, wait around scenic backdrops on the mesa's edge, wait till they get the right light or for the clouds to pass over, let them choose what they want in the background, green forest or distant peaks or stark desert, and say a few lines. Then I wait for my big paycheck, and"—she held up her goblet of Palisade Red—"bring home the free wine."

Luke studied the Book Cliffs, standing at the deck's railing and forcing himself not to get involved in moral arguments. In his mind's eye, he reprised all the roadside fracking operations pocking both sides of Interstate 70 from Vail to Fruita, knowing they were just the visible operations of a huge network drilling into the landscape, spreading north and south deep into the entire Piceance Basin lining the Western Slope of the Rockies. He had enough conservation ethics pondering Jeff's feedlot without taking on fracking, too, which he didn't know enough about anyway.

Right now he didn't want to think about it, didn't want to be Mr. History of Environmental Ethics. He was a guest, here to celebrate Jenn's acting gig and the inauguration of Matt's Horsethief Adventures, to acknowledge the success of the brothers' trial canoe run. He and Matt had finished their scouting at midmorning, celebrating the cottonwood pavilion of bald eagles' nests lining the way to the Westwater take-out. After they'd stored the equipment, Luke had enjoyed the rest of day, taking an easy afternoon solo mountain bike tour in Glade Park while Matt attended to his bike shop.

Luke had been invited to spend even more time in Fruita, but he knew he should hit the road back to Denver in the morning, having left Emily to water the plants and look after Toonces. Jenn and Matt had to return to full workdays—that would be two shifts for Jenn, the commercial shoots and her service at the restaurant, not to mention her summer classes at Mesa College, so he couldn't really hang around anyway. He'd better strap himself to his desk and work on his thesis.

"Baby," Jenn was saying. "Careful. You're doing that thing again, tilting your wine glass."

Matt had scooped up the grilled foods and stood over the platter, his goblet poised to spill over the peppers and steak. He straightened it just in time. "Man, that's so weird. I don't even realize I'm doing it."

"You've got to get that ear checked," Jenn said, going inside to get plates and flatware. "I'm sure that's the culprit. It's knocking you all sideways."

Over dinner, Luke teased Matt about it. "I hope you leave your ear ringing untreated and keep falling out of canoes and stumbling over rocks. When Ted'n'Kathy get home and see it for themselves, they'll realize you're not perfect after all and give me a little credit."

"Oh, poor Lukie. Who's actually their favorite wittle-baby-poo."

"I'm not their favorite, and I never was."

"Luke's right, Matt," Jenn said. "No offense, Luke, but honestly, anyone can see it. Your folks love the hell out of both of you, but Matt's the first son, the most golden of the golden boys."

"Yeah, Ted'n'Kathy do adore you the most. And I'm not making some poor-me observation. I actually kinda like it. It takes the pressure off me. I can hide with my books in tranquility, the family wimp."

"Ha!" Matt cried. "When did you last practice tranquility?"

"I'm just not exuberant like you."

"No, you're smart and dedicated, starting on your master's while I'm a college dropout. Mom and Dad didn't really care for that, if you recall."

"We both need to finish our degrees, Matt, at least before we're forty," Jenn announced, gathering up the plates. "Especially now that I'm going to have in-laws with doctorates, Colorado's foremost experts on endangered species in the Ecuadorian Amazon. I really do have to study my lines, guys. Not for corporate commercials, but my scene study for *Cherry Orchard*. Maybe I can impress Ted'n'Kathy with Chekhov, if not Chevron." With a waitress's practiced agility and aplomb, she balanced the plates while kissing Luke on the forehead, Matt on the lips, thanked him for cooking dinner, and ducked inside.

"Leave the dishes for me," Luke called.

"Oh, they'll be waitin' for ya."

"I sure like her," Luke said, staring at twilight over the cliffs.

"Man, that was a shocker, though." Matt reached for the bottle and refilled both goblets. "I really thought her acting gig was for some environmental public service spot."

"It's like she said, who's gonna pay for that? Can you think of any environmental public service spots you've seen lately? Instead, we've got fossil fuel and fracking dressed up like green saviors."

"Sometimes she thinks so differently from the way we were brought up, Luke. More practical than us Denver greenies."

"She actually sounds pretty conflicted about it."

"But she's still doing it, right?"

"She's a Grand Junction native, isn't she?" Luke asked, feeling called on to defend Jenn, maybe just to slip into his brat little brother role to prove he wasn't a solemn purist. "So she and her family are veterans of booms and busts since her baby days, all those promises that Junction would be the next great Western metropolis, followed by soaped-over storefronts and rental vans packed with families' earthly possessions. After paying tuition whenever she could, raising the money waiting tables, why shouldn't she take a cushy gig for once?"

"Because it's evil?" Matt said, shrugging. Then he laughed. "But the wine's sure nice." He asked Luke if he was still seeing the cowboy.

"Whenever I get a chance. Which ain't as much as I like, with three hundred twenty miles between us."

"Sounds like a real crush, brother."

"It is crushing me."

"So much for books and tranquility, I guess."

❖

"I never much cared for the Fourth of July," Luke told Jeff when they met at the Indian place in River North. "Much ado about fireworks and flag bunting."

"Not very patriotic."

"Oh, I love my country. Just not the pageantry."

"Are you always so complicated? Can't you just join the parade and eat hot dogs? Or tofu dogs, at least?"

"This Indian beer with you is celebration enough. Perfect on a hot midsummer day, huh?" He clinked bottles, grateful Jeff had shown up in Denver for the holiday, a complete surprise. He hadn't expected to see him for another week at the earliest. "So, you have another mysterious meeting tomorrow?"

"I wish it were mysterious. This one's about financials and investors' stakes, my least favorite mission as a cattleman. Stuffy Seventeenth Street boardrooms and hard, detailed questions. But the truth is, I don't have a meeting tomorrow. It's the day after tomorrow. I wanted to spend extra time with you, and I'm just glad you were available, otherwise I would've spent a lot of time pacing my room at the Oxford and watching too much cable news."

Luke absorbed it, smiling but happily devastated. It amounted to a declaration of attachment and a deeper affection than anything either of them had confessed so far. In truth, he was free on the Fourth because of the schism with Marco. Otherwise, he always spent the day with Emily and Gail watching fireworks from her cousin's rooftop in Capitol Hill at a strictly traditional cookout of burgers, corn on the cob, and tofu dogs.

❖

July 5

What I love the most about spending the long holiday weekend with Jeff is that the more I get to know him, the more I like him. He's not only got a brain, but a wide curiosity about history and philosophy, and he's helped me formulate some of my vague ideas for the thesis into something that addresses history and philosophy, specifically where ethical principles and history converge.

He probed my thoughts about my scattered research into the Summitville disaster, how it goes so much farther back into history than a 1980s Superfund cleanup site. The degradation goes back millions of years to natural acidification and on to the earliest days of European settlement, when early mines worsened the watershed by exposing the surface to weathering, leaching metals into the runoff.

Jeff wanted to know the grim details about how the last owners, the Canadian speculators who used cyanide to extract gold from ore in the 1980s, abandoned the mines. They only paid a fraction of the cleanup, leaving the US taxpayers to pay $155 million more, while three thousand gallons of contaminated water leaked from the site per minute. For two years in the early 90s, aquatic life vanished along seventeen miles of the Alamosa River.

Jeff wanted to know how the whole shebang could be analyzed in utilitarian terms. He was so intrigued by the moral questions of the Canadian corporation's culpability that he exhausted my store of knowledge. He inspired me to hit the research deeper. It makes me want to explore this relationship deeper, too. I've never known this kind of mental rigor with a man of interest.

I'm more than interested.

❖

"Marco's completely shut me out," Luke told Matt when they video-chatted two nights before Matt's maiden canoe guide. "I didn't even get to watch his team win the swimming relays."

"Did you remind him that you taught him how to swim?"

Luke struggled to keep Toonces in his lap and his paws

off the keyboard. "I haven't had a chance. Gail and Emily can force him to stay at the table or sit in the same room with me, but no one can force him to communicate with me. It stinks."

"I'm sorry, Luke. It's gotta hurt."

"Yeah, a lot. Meanwhile, Emily says he hankers for you and feels cheated the normal brother abandoned him."

"But you were always closest, Lukie, his best champion. I can't believe he's become such a homophobic little shit." Toonces punctuated Matt's disgust by tapping Luke's keyboard and making the screen go jumpy. Long before his move to the Western Slope, Matt had helped with Luke's father-subbing, coaching Marco in the basics of Little League baseball while Luke concentrated on Tadpole aquatics. The brothers double-teamed to backstop the fatherless boy and had basked in Marco's gratitude and esteem until now.

"Anyway, what did your doc say?"

"He's Jenn's doctor, remember? I don't have a doctor."

"You do now. Come on, cut the stalling. Tell me."

"He doesn't like how the tinnitus is just in one ear. He had me do a couple simple balance exercises, right there in his damn office hallway. I kind of flunked, okay? I couldn't even walk heel to toe without practically falling over."

"So, does he agree that the tinnitus is messing up your balance, or what?"

"He wasn't sure. He's scheduled an MRI right after I get off the river."

"For what? To find a big old broken incandescent light bulb rattling in your ear canal?"

"Exactly. They're going to see if can they screw in a compact fluorescent to help save the planet. And me."

❖

July 8

183 lbs. 32 laps

While Matt is swimming with his family group from their camp at Black Rocks on the sandy banks of the Colorado River, laughing down the rapids, I'm doing monotonous laps at the Congress Park pool. Practically the minute the guards whistle the lappers out, and with barely twelve seconds to rinse off, great hordes of daycare kids who've been lining up crash the gates. As I lie there on the concrete, drying off in the hot sun, the tsunami of kid noise is almost unbearable. As happy as it is, it's so loud I gotta get out of there without even bothering to check out any cute adult personages in Speedos elsewhere on the pool deck. So it's not exactly a frolic on the Colorado River, but I do always feel great afterward, especially when I think about my summer freedom, and it's infinitely better than cramming down a sandwich in the teachers' crusty work room on some godforsaken wintry noon during the school year.

This afternoon, though, I had to meet with my substitute thesis advisor in a crusty work room on campus. Grumpy was crusty himself, as usual, barely able to hide his aversion to me. He also seemed unaware Dr. Buster Levine, my real true advisor and fellowship director of my semester of teaching college freshmen, had already approved my topic before his leave of absence. Or maybe Grumpy disapproved of Buster's approval, too. Grumpy certainly seemed less impressed than he was before with my idea about the intersection of history and environmental ethics at the Summitville disaster.

"So far, it sounds a bit light on both history and ethics," he pronounced. He seemed to find my dabbling in Peter Singer vs. Leo Strauss déclassé or even gauche. He wondered how Strauss's stress on natural rights and political engagement specifically intersected with a seeping disaster of toxins in Southern Colorado. Grumpy thought I would find more relevance applying Peter Singer's bioethics, his utilitarian or practical ethics. "But trying to trick up some opposition between Strauss and Singer on Summitville? I worry, Mr. Devlin."

Now I'm worried. I didn't dare mention existentialist ethics, which tend to leave me in a muddle in my most clear moments, let alone at the mercy of a skeptical professor. I know advisors have to play the devil's advocate so grad students don't get lost in ill-considered theses. But Jesus, a little encouragement might also help me.

Still, I'm drawn to the drama of Summitville, the whole notion of that mountaintop's steady abuse since the European settlement of Colorado, then its ravaging by modern corporations injecting poisons into its low-grade ore. It unleashed hell on an entire watershed just for a little hard-won gold. Not to mention the corporation being unable to pay for the mess it made or being willing and capable of ever really healing the wound. I don't want this particular disaster or its moral hazards ever to be forgotten.

❖

"I brought my first guided tour off, but just barely," Matt reported when he got off the river. "I just can't hear right with that damn tinnitus. It's a disaster waiting to happen on the river when I can't hear the clients."

"How close to a real disaster?" Luke asked, sure Matt was exaggerating. On the family patio with his tablet, he stared at the ancient oak he and Matt used to climb, lit by the little yard lights strung branch to branch. Over their mother's plans to dismantle it, the brothers' crude treehouse was preserved due to their pleading that it was a Family Historical Site. "What the hell happened, Matt?"

"Well, I didn't capsize and neither did anyone in the party. These folks were all decent paddlers, ideal for my first clients. Independent without being obnoxious, but obedient about river rules and smart about their kids' boundaries. Really great—I loved 'em. It was me. I came close to another swim at the Black Rocks rapids because I was straining to hear what the mom was yelling to me about her kids' canoe. I turned and almost flipped straight overboard. Thank God one of the older kids was up front—he righted the canoe just fine and we glided straight to shore. Nobody knew, thank God, and I was able to fake it when I couldn't hear their questions or comments. But I've got to figure out how to improve this before the next trip."

"After a couple broken-glass incidents here at the condo, we just bought a set of plastic tumblers." Jenn squeezed on the screen, sitting on the arm of Matt's deck chair. "He's more motivated and serious about the MRI now. But we've got to pay for it all ourselves, because Matt's health insurance is high deductible. A couple thousand bucks."

"Thank God Jenn's become a movie star."

Jenn laughed. "The money is good for these thirty-second spots. But bad for soul-killing bullshit on behalf of big energy."

"I say thank God for soul-killing bullshit," Matt said.

"Not to mention," Luke said, "the diagnostic powers of magnetic resonance imaging."

❖

July 11

I persuaded Jeff to stay at the house for his visit to Denver this week. So, it's been weird the last couple nights, making love with Jeff in my boyhood bedroom, on the worn-out double bed I slept in from middle school through college. Luckily we could scream, groan, and laugh as much as we wanted without alarming anyone, while Toonces, blasé, wandered over our writhing bodies. We wore out that worn-out old mattress even more, but it still felt vaguely sinful. I don't know why, since I don't believe in sin.

As for Jeff, he loves our old, rambling place on Vine Street along with the rest of the neighborhood. Weirdly, he didn't want to sample Liks ice cream. I thought it was an essential intro to our neighborhood rituals, but he said the lines were too long. We enjoyed Cheesman Park after dark, marveling at the guys still cruising each other in their cars. Maybe it's just the heat wave's impact, but I thought these old school hookups had died off with social media.

I told Jeff how Matt used to take me over to the playground when we were little, so Jeff had to check it out, trying out the swing set, both of us stirring the warm air under the faint city stars. I said the constellations must be crazy bright up in Wyoming. You've got to see it for yourself, he said, even the Northern Lights on rare occasions.

So I said, well, invite me.

He just laughed. Did I really need an invitation at this point?

Hell yes, I told him, now that his feedlot security guard has it out for me like I'm some kind of vegetarian activist.

Aren't you? I've been reading up on your bioethics guy, Peter Singer. The father of modern animal rights. Cattlemen aren't exactly his children of virtue.

Don't look at me. I'm just a humble grad student. I don't have a bull in your fight with Singer.

That's when he propelled off his swing, graceful as a kid, and grabbed me to stop my sway by pulling me into a kiss. I had that same feeling I had making love with him in my bed, the inauguration of that mattress for the first time, a grownup at last. Now I was making out with him in my childhood playground in the dark. I loved everything about him, his faint aftershave, strong back, his chiseled chin and shapely cowboy butt. But it was more than the draw of lust. It was the bedazzlement of love, I think, because I just wanted to be with him with or without the promise of anything more.

He held me, whispering that he was afraid this was getting serious, wasn't it? Was it too soon, after just a month, to talk about love?

I was freaked out, because I didn't dream his feelings were as strong as mine. So I said something slightly smartass like, "In my experience, it's usually too soon. But I don't have much experience."

He didn't laugh the way I expected.

❖

When Jeff got back from his cattlemen's association board meeting the next afternoon, Luke sensed something had changed. Jeff had bought flowers downtown, since they were bound for Gail's birthday party, but now after a whole day of policy discussion, he wondered if there would be a lot of people there. When Luke assured him it was a small, informal evening barbecue on the patio with some cake and champagne he was bringing, Jeff still seemed to balk.

It was just a few blocks along Twelfth Avenue across Josephine into Capitol Heights, bearing the bubbly and Jeff's gorgeous, gaudy bouquet, but the silence seemed to harden, matching Jeff's sulky mood. After two speechless blocks, Luke asked if it was too soon to start meeting each other's old friends. "Do you feel I'm, like, pressuring you to meet my best friend and her mom?"

"No, that's not it. It's really the opposite. I want to know about your life, meet your friends and family, everything. Remember what I asked you last night in the playground? I'm just not sure I want to keep going on with this if you're not as serious as I am. Because, okay." He stared ahead, grim. "I think I'm falling in love."

Luke waited for the green light to cross York Street, absorbing the words. He wasn't hesitant or apprehensive and realized immediately Jeff had misinterpreted his self-satire last night as indifference or a blitheness Luke didn't feel at all. He knew exactly what he needed to say.

Across York, past the traffic, Luke stopped walking and tugged on Jeff's arm. Standing on an old flagstone pavement, Luke plucked a rose from the bouquet. "I didn't say anything last night because I was absorbing what you said. I couldn't really say I was falling in love because I already love you. So, I can't fall because I've already fallen, Jeff." He handed him the rose. "I love you, damn it."

They walked on the last blocks without speaking. For Luke, it was a joyful, almost ecstatic silence. Jeff just paced forward, bearing the rose and the bouquet with a stunned expression. There were stacks of bedding plants in front of the hardware store, fledgling but withered marigolds and picked-over petunias unwanted in mid-July. Luke positioned the champagne against his side and pulled Jeff into a kiss between the stacks. "Knocked ya speechless, didn't I? Good. Gotcha, cowpoke."

The two men reached Gail and Emily's door in the glow of Luke's revelations. One of Emily's young cousins met them in the foyer, exhorting Luke with a blurted comment about "your-brother-Matt's-girlfriend!" then hurried back to the den, where Gail, Emily, Marco, and a few close relatives were gathered around the TV.

"Jenn is amazing," Gail was saying, waving them in, pointing at the screen. "I don't know what it is, but it's so compelling. Especially for a commercial!"

"She's pretty but nonthreatening," Emily was saying. "She's smart, but not smart-alecky. And her character makes fun of the evil corporations she works for."

All three of the first released commercials were in rotation on a local TV newsmagazine. In this one, a full minute long, Jenn's character, Vanessa the Environmental Geologist, is hiking a pine-fringed rim of Grand Mesa with her young daughter and a friend, who recites negative facts about fracking.

"Of course big corporations have ravaged our western landscapes," Vanessa answers as her little girl climbs up into her embrace. "And they have forever. Look at the century-old waste left behind by that mine we just explored. But come on, Kate, do you think I could bear to do this work if I didn't think hydrologic fracturing was different?" Vanessa's light, friendly tone becomes dead serious as her daughter shyly hides her face against her shoulder. "How could I bear to be a part of damaging what's left of our wild places for this one here?" she says, hoisting the girl to look out at the vista, the Book Cliffs and the Monument beckoning on the sun-drenched horizon. "Or anyone's kids? Kate, I'm doing this for them."

"Yeah, she's scary good," Emily's uncle said as he started outside to join the party around the backyard barbecue. "Notice she never once said what she is doing."

"What she is doing is damaging what's left of our wild places and destroying the Earth for her daughter and lying about it while smiling through those gorgeous white choppers," Emily said, hugging Luke and then meeting Jeff's extended hand with a hug. "And speaking of gorgeous! No wonder Luke is gaga over you."

"I'm not that gaga. And don't embarrass my boyfriend."

"The flowers are brilliant, Jeff," Gail said, bussing his cheek while cradling the bouquet. "Welcome to Luke's other family."

"See how easy they are?" Luke said to Jeff. "You could be a mass murderer, but a handsome face makes Emily and Gail weak in the knees."

"You make me sick," Marco announced, exiting the room through the sliding glass door to the yard.

"Oy," Luke said. "I didn't realize Marco was still there."

"It doesn't matter," Emily said. "He's just being stubborn."

"Still, I didn't mean to flaunt it in front of Marco."

"Please, just be yourselves," Gail said, still smiling at Jeff. "Like I said, you're family here, and I'm thrilled to have you. Marco is going to come around when he's good and ready. Now," she added, gesturing with the bouquet toward the patio, "let's all go outside, throw some more meat on the barbecue, and make fun of Lukie's little tofu dog!"

❖

July 13

> jogged 2 x around Cheesman path
> 24 laps at Congress Pool
> 182 lbs!

It's hot, hot, hot, that inevitable July heat wave that sits on the city like an obese, immovable, unwelcome guest. After noon laps, I stake out a space in the pool's deep end even while the daycare tykes explode through the gates. I stay, enduring the wall of noise just for the relief of dunking myself in semi-cool water and avoiding the frying pan sizzle of the pool deck.

This is the only time I've really yearned to have my little apartment back, just for the A/C. Mom and Dad always claimed they didn't need it for the house because the upstairs fans going day and night did the trick, and besides, "the heat's only unbearable in Denver for one lousy week every summer." Or ten days. Or maybe a month. I look for excuses to take the car for errands just to run the air conditioner, and I linger over the seafood at King Soopers to stare at the ice and prolong the sterile supermarket frigidity.

Summer vacation's fully ripe now, over half gone. I don't know what this journal is eventually going to reveal about time's passage, but I do know this particular summer has peaked beautifully. Not even the heat can sink the cloud marked number nine that I'm riding across July skies. The more time I spend with Jeff, the more it feels like the real thing, making me realize I've never known what that was until now. The only problem is those 321 miles I've wanted to cross as soon as he returned home to Wyoming this morning. I keep thinking how cool it would be with Jeff again at that cabin in the Black Hills, and the easy coupling we could practice to keep warm up there at night.

After he left this morning, I felt desolate and numb, reading endless accounts of the Summitville disaster with the fan in my face and the gorgeous cerulean sky in the window like a temptation to come out and play. That's the yin and yang of this crazy feeling, that's the price I pay—this pattern of short, intense connections and longer, bewildered spells of missing him. It's all happened so fast, barely a month, that I can't really process it. I just try to cope with those waves as they materialize and then overtake me, not a familiar feat for a landlocked Rocky Mountain kid who's hoping not to drown in his own stupid happiness.

❖

"You should've seen the look on the MRI technician's face. I don't think she knew I was watching her in her booth, through that little mirror," Matt told Luke, laughing. "Her mouth was wide open with astonishment, like a cartoon."

"I'm not getting the humor, brother." The call came late in the evening, later than Matt usually called, just as Luke was getting ready to join Damien at Aunt Pete's. "This sounds pretty serious."

"It is, I know, but if you don't laugh about it, it'll drive you crazy. Nobody told me the MRI was going to rattle and shake and make loud, insane noises for almost an hour. They originally told me a half hour but decided to run another session, 'with contrast' or something. The racket is like you're inside a space capsule that's being struck on all sides by random artillery."

"What did the doc say about the results?"

"That extra half hour doubled the price, by the way. Naturally."

"I can help you with that, Matt, don't worry about it." Luke knew Matt was stalling, a family trait about bad news. He took his phone to the deck and sat down. The pear and plum trees shuddered together in a sudden gust. Under them, one of the solar yard lights had flickered out. "What did the doc say?"

"Well, he thinks it's a tumor. Like, in the right side of my brain."

"Jesus!"

"It needs more diagnosis. He's not sure exactly what to do with this type of tumor. They've got to run more tests. Of course, they've got to run up the bill. The doc in Grand Junction wants me to see a neurologist in their Denver hospital. He's already set up an appointment."

"How are you feeling?"

"I'm fine, Lukie. Same as ever. Don't I sound fine? Did I tell you about the kkkkkkkk's I've been making on the keyboard, pressing my middle finger on the 'k' key without meaning to? Something new, out of the blue. I just hope I don't accidently hit it only three times anytime anyone is watching. Just what I need, being accused of white supremacy. I can just hear Damien—"

"Matt, you might have bigger worries. Really, no pain at all?"

"There hasn't been any serious pain, just those little

headaches now and then. Two ibuprofen always do the trick, so it can't be that bad, right?"

"Matt, come on. Is it malignant?"

"Seriously, they don't know."

"So, they're gonna run a biopsy?"

"I guess. Jenn's family physician, who went over the MRI scan, was mostly concerned about the size of the thing. That's why the technician was freaked. So, here's the good news. I've had this thing in my brain for years, maybe since I was a teenager."

"That's the good news?"

"Well, it hasn't caused me any problems so far, that's all I mean. It's like an old friend. We've learned to live together all this time, right? My tumor and me."

Luke sighed. "Besides the headaches and the 'k's and your lack of balance, what else are you noticing?"

"Have you ever thought of going into medicine? You sound just like this doctor."

"Come off it. He's already scheduled a neurology appointment in Denver. They're not messing around."

"No, they're not." Matt's tone changed, the lightness slipping out. He sounded frustrated now. "The balance is getting worse, for sure. Like in the shower just now."

"What happened?"

"I slipped against the glass door. Almost cracked the damn thing, okay? I broke the fall by reaching for the edge of the bathtub, but I kind of screwed up my right arm. It hurts a little, like I pulled a muscle. It'll be okay by tomorrow."

"When are you coming?"

"Luckily Jenn's working late tonight, so she didn't have to see me floundering around naked in the shower like a spastic three-year-old. Did I tell you she's headed to Pittsburgh to shoot a whole new series of fracking commercials out there?

For their local markets? She's so popular in Colorado and Wyoming, they want to export her to Pennsylvania."

"That's great for Jenn, but when are you coming to Denver, brother?"

❖

July 15

Matt is going to be here tomorrow for his consult with the neurologist. He wants to stay overnight, make his morning appointment, and head back to Fruita from there. He's got to get everything ready for his next canoe clients, putting in on the river on the eighteenth.

I didn't really feel like going out after Matt's call, but Damien had already showed up to walk with me down to Aunt Pete's. I kept reviewing Matt's words, how evasive and jokey he was about something so critical, which was typical, but this was extreme even for him. Is the tumor starting to affect his cognition? Are his doctors not exactly sure what to do? Anticipating the neurologist's diagnosis started to consume all my thoughts.

I was not very good company for Damien and didn't want to get into it with him. He chattered away as we reached Colfax, excited about some cute guy who'd just joined his hospice nursing team and agreed to meet him at Aunt Pete's for a beer. I half listened, wary as we strolled among the Colfax characters the heat had brought out, especially a small mob of retro-looking skinheads in black shitkickers and ripped T-shirts. The biggest of their roving troupe wolf-whistled when Damien and I sidled by in front of an Irish brewpub. The other punks all laughed. When Damien whispered, "Maybe the big guy thinks we're cute," I steered him away, grabbing his scrawny elbow. He said he didn't need protection. "You're not my great white savior."

"No, I'm your great white friend. Who would hate to see you get hurt again."

He just said, "I can handle racists myself."

"That would be reassuring if you didn't have the physique of a rickety twelve-year-old. That guy thinks we're fagmeat, ripe for carving up." I was glad we were almost at Aunt Pete's, where a burly bouncer guarded the doorway.

My heart sank when we hurried inside. It was pretty dead, no more than twenty or so guys scattered around the whole place, most of them clustered close to the outdoor bar.

A dark thought crossed my mind that if things didn't work out with Jeff, I'd be reduced to hanging around this place again, and I couldn't stand that or scrolling through online sites and apps if I didn't want to live by myself for the next several decades. Before I died alone, of course, in some fussy old queers' home.

After we ordered drinks, Damien immediately found his new crush from work and left me at the bar to sip my vodka tonic alone and contemplate how depressing the place is when it's so empty—shabby, smelling of stale beer and alcoholic desperation. It was the last place I wanted to be after my call from Matt, and I was just about to signal to Damien that I was going to take off when his skinny acquaintance approached me, the one who'd asked me about "the cowboy" back in June. "Have you had the full Jeffrey Douglas Experience yet, buddy? The cabin in the Black Hills, the empty Indian restaurant in River North?"

I wasn't in the mood for snark. I just nodded.

"And you're what, about a month into it, so he keeps coming to Denver for business meetings and might even have declared his love?" To my surprise, the skinny guy didn't crack a sardonic smile or affect a theatrical tone. He just made the case with a practiced weariness. "Well, have fun while it lasts, doll, but be careful. If history is any guide, in a few weeks he'll be crying on your shoulder about how stranded he is up on the historic Thunder Creek Family Ranch and whether you wouldn't mind sharing him with his wife."

Damien distracted us, pulling the nurse guy into an introduction and saying how glad he was that the skinny guy and I had become friends. Before I knew where, the skinny guy had disappeared.

❖

"You don't really know the skinny messenger," Emily said. "It could all be complete BS."

"Except that he knew about the cabin and the empty Indian place, remember?" Luke said. The two of them walked their traditional summer evening route, grabbing coffees at the café inside Tattered Cover, then across Colfax to the Esplanade. When they passed the East High School baseball diamond, where some summer league was practicing in the twilight, Luke thought of all the hours spent watching Matt's games when he was a shortstop during their championship season, his senior year. He wasn't bad at bat, either, scoring a few home runs. Sprinting over the bases, did he already have a tumor growing inside that seventeen-year-old brain?

The batter on the diamond cracked a nice one over the right fielder's raised mitt and made it as far as second base. The sound forced Luke's memory back to all the times they'd played catch with Marco after dinner when he was just starting Little League. On leaving Emily's place this evening, Marco had turned down a chance to walk with the two of them to the park for the first time ever. Emily had chalked it up to his getting too big for his britches now that he was going into seventh grade.

Luke didn't believe that, but he didn't want to talk about Marco's ongoing homophobic snit any more than he wanted to talk about being Jeff Douglas's dupe and clueless partner in adultery, but Emily wanted to know more. Of course.

"Okay," Luke theorized, "it's clear Jeff doesn't want anyone in Denver seeing him out with a strange guy."

"And you're plenty strange."

"Thanks, dear. He has lots of family and business associates here, and he's keeping his boyfriends on the down low. That locked closet in the cabin was probably full of his wife's clothes. And there was a weird moment up there when I passed him a magazine he wanted to read, and he tore off the label first thing. Now I understand. He didn't want to forget and have his wife or kids ask him who Lucas Devlin is and why Jeff has his copy of *Harper's*."

"You still don't know if he really has a wife, let alone kids."

"When I drove by the ranch, two boys were playing on the lawn of the main house."

"They could've been anyone's boys. Ranch hands' sons. Random locals."

"Thanks for trying."

"I just don't want you to give up completely. I really like Jeff, and you two seemed perfect together."

"Argh! Right now I'd like to corner him on some crowded night at Aunt Pete's and empty a cocktail in his face, like in some old movie, then let him know exactly what a creep I think he is."

"Put the revenge fantasy on hold for a while, at least until you learn the whole truth."

"Not to mention it'd be a waste of a perfectly good cocktail."

By the time they crossed Seventeenth Avenue into City Park, Luke knew he had to change the subject, not only because it make him heartsick to talk any more about Jeff, but he sure didn't want to mention Matt's health yet. So he slipped into silence, strolling beside the green, tree-dotted expanse filled with dog walkers, picnickers, lovers, and laughing kids. A thunderstorm had burst over the city in the late afternoon, cooling down the ninety-five-plus inferno. Rain puddles shimmered in the last glimpses of sun setting over the mountains.

"My God. It's midsummer already." Emily stopped walking for a moment as if to inhale the evening's green breeziness. "How's your journal project going? I imagine, up until your debacle at Aunt Pete's, you've chronicled every perfect day."

"I've been pretty faithful, most days. But even with the entries, the summer still seems to slip out of reach. You just can't save the days. They vanish no matter how consciously you spend them. They vanish *because* you spend them. I go to my first teachers' meeting in less than a month."

"Poor thing. I'm dreaming of taking a three-day weekend sometime in August, maybe stowing myself away on one of Matt's guided canoe trips down Horsethief Canyon."

"That'd be great. You can talk to him about it tomorrow." Luke mentioned Matt was coming to Denver for an over-nighter, then wished he hadn't, because Emily got all excited and started asking him for updates on all things Matt. Damn.

"What's the matter, Luke? Why aren't you glad he's coming?"

Damn. Emily knew him too well. "I am." Luke tried to smile a big fake grin. "See?"

"Don't tell me the Perfect Brothers had a fight." She looked at him, gasping a little at whatever expression Luke couldn't hide. "You didn't! Did you?"

"No. Listen, Em. I know he'd love to have you along on one of his Horsethief adventures. I wasn't going to tell you this until his neurology consult tomorrow." As they roamed the rose garden radiating from the pavilion on Ferril Lake, he told her what he knew, stressing how long Matt had already lived with the tumor and how it was probably benign. "He sounds good on the phone, same old Matt joking around, so it's probably not one of those malignant monsters that overtake people so fast."

Emily stared at a tall clump of canna, her arms wrapped around her chest. Robotic, hushed, she said, "Ever notice how the crimson ones seem to hold the light, even after the sun sets?"

"Yeah, it's getting dark. Come on, I'll walk you back home. I really didn't mean to bring this up yet. I was gonna wait until he got his results. I'm sorry."

"Lucas Devlin, stop apologizing. Be a real gentleman and give me a hug right now." Emily pulled him into one, leaning her head on his chest and shoulder. "I would've killed you if you hadn't told me."

❖

July 17

Matt's sleeping now. I just checked on him, snoozing in his room. I usually wouldn't invade his privacy, but everything seems different now. He looks and acts different than even a few weeks ago. The right side of his face seems tighter somehow, pushing his smile leftward and making him talk more from the left side of his mouth. Meanwhile his right eye is weird, not always blinking along with his left, like it's on a delay. At least he looked comfortable— and his face more symmetrical—while snoring away.

When he got here in the late afternoon, Matt's new symptoms freaked me out, something I hope I disguised, like when he told me about his drive over the mountains on I-70. He prides himself on being a good driver, so it had to be hard to admit how scary this crossing must have been. He said he couldn't shake this irrational tendency to pull left into the next lane, and if he was in the left lane, to swerve into the median.

"I even let go of the steering wheel," he said, "on straight flat stretches to see if the alignment was cattywampus, but it was fine. It was coming from me, my own grip. Thank God it was four divided lanes the whole way. What would it be like to fight that rightward tug on two-lane blacktop? It wasn't suicidal or homicidal, Lukie, just an inescapable temptation. I had to keep fighting it, righting the steering wheel as if it had its own determination. For four freaking hours."

So, I'll make sure I drive Matt to the neurologist's tomorrow morning. I'm sure he'll provide some answers on the sudden bad behavior of this tumor and a positive course of treatment. I've switched from researching Summitville to brain tumors, and tonight found myself clicking link to link about things like alpha knives and stun guns in research hospitals as far flung as San Diego and Montreal. For now, though, I'm going to concentrate on Denver having the answers that Grand Junction believed it wasn't equipped to make.

❖

Luke spent the early morning worrying about getting Matt ready after his brother's long deep sleep. He made breakfast for the groggy, miserable slug-a-bed and then made sure they were on time for the midmorning neurology appointment.

Matt wanted to walk, insisting on the Devlin propensity to be green, never driving any walkable or bikeable distance. Freshly showered, hair combed, and smiling on the front porch, arrayed as if for the first day of school in a baby blue button-down tucked into a pair of ancient khakis he'd found in his room, Matt declared, "It's a beautiful morning." Of course it was. Like most July mornings in Denver, the sparkling blue sky was free even of the little clouds that, later, would cross east to west like scouts for what Matt called the daily "thunder threats."

They paced straight north on Vine Street, following the familiar route they took almost every morning of their high school years. Would that they were walking to whatever first hour had to offer, Luke basking in the reflected glory of his cool, magnanimous brother, and not on this terrible errand.

Except Matt the schoolboy had also been exquisite in coordination and self-possession. Now sometimes dragging his left foot and tripping at odd intervals, his brother kept cursing the upended flagstone pavers under some of the most ancient trees. "The city really ought to get after these sidewalk slackers." Even on flat concrete stretches, Matt knocked into Luke's shoulder, veering left on foot just like he described he'd done behind the wheel. Crossing Sixteenth Avenue, Luke realized walking on Matt's right stopped him from colliding, though at one point Matt swerved off the sidewalk completely and trampled somebody's marigolds.

Just down the block, a school friend popped out on a front porch, holding up a baby in a blue blanket, blinking into the morning sun. "Son, hail our senior president! Matt Devlin!"

"Looks like you've been busy, Joe."

"Yeah, Maggie and I spent the last year bringing this little dude into the world. Just dropping him off at my mom's. Where ya going, guys?"

"A morning walk," Matt said. "Just another deposed president surveying his vanished domain."

The doctor's office was only ten blocks away but a world unknown. With grandparents far away or gone before he was born, Luke had grown up into the healthy, deathless precincts of white, middle-class America where emergency rooms and funerals existed only as backdrops for movies and TV dramas. He was well aware of the health care building boom walling off the north end of Uptown but barely knew which hospital was which. Their appointment was in the office tower adjacent to the posh-resort Catholic-Jewish hospital. A concierge in a dark suit directed them to the elevators.

Waiting for the lift to the sixth floor, Luke realized he hadn't prepared himself. The air of luxury was immediately undermined by clusters of hobbling folks exiting the elevators, burdened and bent over, steadying themselves on walkers, minding their oxygen, stepping gingerly on wounded legs, bearing portable fluid bags or combinations of all these while attended by worried relatives or determined assistants. It was like a sad, geriatric army had taken over a grand hotel and discharged its wounded from lost battles.

Dr. Leibniz, the lead neurosurgeon, led the brothers into a cave-like office with vast wall-mounted screens. Dr. Nilsson, the radiology surgeon, was already studying the screens, shaking hands as he indicated the multiple views of Matt's cranium on display.

Tall, around sixty, Leibniz was intense under his proud mane of slicked-back dark hair. He didn't try to hide his ardent fascination with the case, almost congratulating Matt on the mind-blowing size of the tumor. "First the good news. The biopsy shows no malignant cancerous growth. Of course, there is always a chance it could metastasize. It could be Matt's extreme fitness and youth forestalled the inevitable symptoms all this time." Leibnitz seemed to be theorizing for the benefit of his consulting partner. "It might even be that Matt's athletics and robust health encouraged his toleration for the tumor's massive growth over the past ten years, which probably has been very slow and steady until expanding just recently."

He mouse-clicked through the multiple MRI images until he settled on a side view. "Here's where I'm most concerned."

He gestured for the three to crowd closer to the oversized computer screen. Under the soft gray tissue of his cerebellum, the large ball of a brighter gray tumor bulged around the top of his spinal cord. A kind of tail wrapped itself around a whiter stub, dead center. Leibnitz gestured around it, circling the cord-like line between the spine and tumor with the eraser of his pencil.

"Right here," he said. "Around the brain stem, a glioma. Unusually attached and spreading, it's this coiling, snake-like wiggle. I would love to get in there and scoop out the tumor surgically—I've done 'em by the hundreds—but this one makes me hesitate. It's too enveloped with the stem. As the tumor presses closer against it, basic functionality could be severely compromised."

Dr. Nilsson, younger and much smaller than his colleague, thin and pale, seemed to be the yang to Leibniz's yin. "I'm curious," he asked Matt in a soft, shy way, "have you had double vision or nausea?"

"Neither!" Matt asserted, as if proud. "Is it possible it's not really that severe?"

"More like it's amazing," Leibniz said. "So far, you're doing much better than we'd expect."

"Can I just go on living with this, then?"

Leibniz and Nilsson exchanged glances. "We recommend going forward with treatment," Leibniz said. "At this point, the best option is a course of radiation. Right away."

"But nothing is guaranteed, Matt," Dr. Nilsson hurried to add. "You must understand."

"But doing nothing isn't an option," Leibniz said, more to Nilsson than Matt.

"We hope to shrink the tumor and contain it before it reaches the brain stem. That's our best hope."

Luke felt the heavy impression Nilsson was trying to convince himself, too.

"Okay," Matt said, as if closing the deal on a set of sketchy new tires. "Can I undergo the treatments back in Grand Junction? I was hoping to get back to my bike shop as soon as I could."

This time, the surgeons traded longer glances in a prolonged silence. "We can only do this course of radiation therapy right here at our main Denver facility," Nilsson said. "We're hoping you can devote a month, about an hour Monday through Friday, to your treatments. Is that going to be possible?"

"A *month*?" Matt tried to absorb it, mentioning his bike shop demands and his planned weekend guided tours. "It's the very height of high season. Can I get by until the fall?"

"I understand you're worried about managing your business, Matt," Leibniz said. "A month is a long time. But I have to be blunt. This is much bigger than making a living in your bike shop."

"This is about saving your life," Nilsson said.

"Let's hope you have staff who can manage things at your shop," Leibniz said. "And a place to stay while you're in Denver."

"We're both Denverites, staying ten blocks from here at our parents' place for the summer," Luke said. "We could easily arrange an hour a day."

"I thought I was crashing in Denver one night for this appointment. I didn't realize I was *staying* here," Matt said, half smiling.

"You are now," Luke said, not smiling at all.

❖

July 19

We went straight out of Leibniz's cave with Dr. Nilsson, who led us through the new, marble-columned perfect purgatory next door into the Radiology department. He was so short and compact between Matt and me, like a Boy Scout volunteer taking us on a guided tour to earn his medical merit badge. Squeezed between the new hospital and the old one still being demolished, Radiology occupied a sterile, emptied 1980s facility. Defying the vacancy, workmen in dust-covered overalls took their breaks in jumbled seats in the vast empty space between old and new, as if purgatory's sanitized waiting room had recently imploded. I had a bad feeling. Everything felt improvisational and moveable, like a stage set for a hospital drama series that had been unexpectedly canceled.

It seemed like Nilsson walked us through five or six sliding glass doors to a small consulting room somewhere in the innards of Radiology, every wall advertising warnings about exposure or nuclear waste disposal or pointing the way to emergency exits. There was hesitancy about Nilsson, a pause-heavy decorum, as if he was holding back.

Matt just sat on the examination bed, looking beat down and sleepless despite his marathon snooze. Into the bright fluorescent silence I blundered onward, shamelessly summarizing my online research about the magic Alpha Wand in San Diego and the amazing Gamma Gun in Montreal, or vice versa.

I figured Nilsson would be irritated, but he didn't roll his eyes or rush to minimize my input. Instead, his sad eyes looked even more pained. He explained calmly that the Alpha Wand and many other touted high-tech anti-tumor methodology was pretty much identical to the equipment footsteps away in their radiology lab. He tried to smile.

"I just want you both to know that I agree with Dr. Leibniz's assessment completely. And how highly I regard his diagnostic accuracy. I wish we could've begun a course of radiation months ago but, Matt, you've been so asymptomatic for so long."

"Sorry, Doc. Up until I started tripping on my own feet a few weeks ago, I thought I was the healthiest guy on the planet."

Matt was led away to be measured for some kind of mask to hold his head in place during treatments, and Nilsson, briefly touching my arm, showed me a doorway behind cheery fabric curtains and excused himself with that sad smile, indicating the Male Waiting Room, adjacent to an inner dressing room. Under a flatscreen running sports news updates, three older women occupied the narrow space. "Oh my, an actual male." They laughed. "And young!"

Feeling old, I tried to joke back. "How did your gender reassignment surgery go?"

"What do you think?" the boldest one said, laughing. One woman with a headscarf, not like a hijab but a bright, tight silk wrapping, joined in the laughter and tried to speak, but it was inaudible. The bold one said, "Yeah, Aren't we a bunch of gorgeous old broads?"

"Gorgeous," I agreed, wondering whether I would get to know these women occupying the Male Waiting Room in the coming days, and for how long.

❖

July 20

Luke had arrived at the Rocky Mountain Brewing Company early to get an outdoor table right next to the heavy noon foot traffic of the Sixteenth Street Mall. When Jeff arrived in dark glasses and a long-visored cap, he tried to sit with his back to the mall, but Luke interrupted his effort with a sideways hug that was barely reciprocated.

"Here, take my seat instead," Luke said. "I thought your aged visage in the sunny glare would shock me, but you're handsome as ever. I mean, what I can make of you under the cap and shades."

"Thanks. I guess that's a compliment. So, you have company at the house? Your brothers, did you say?"

"Just the only brother I've got." When Jeff had announced his unexpected arrival in Denver, having caught a flight out of Lusk with another cattlemen's board member, Luke made it clear that Jeff couldn't stay with him on Vine Street. Now he drank deep of his wheat lager, savoring the taste of this set-up scenario much too much. His burning anger for vengeance had cooled to a mere thirst for prolonged torture. "Matt. The one and only."

"The Fruita bike guy with the TV actress girlfriend, right?"

"Yep. Right now his girlfriend's working back east."

"How open are you with him?"

"You mean, does my brother know I'm queer?" Luke raised his voice a bit. "Of course, dude! We're wild and crazy twenty-first-century guys. Oh my God, he knew before I did, back when I was hardly more than a little gay rug rat. He's always been the one who has to endure my tales of betrayal at the hands of yet another unscrupulous, unsavory loser."

Jeff raised his eyebrows and flashed a puzzled smile. Luke enjoyed drawing out the mystery of what Jeff must be wondering: *If it's just your brother, then why the hell can't we fuck our brains out in your bedroom?*

"I guess—I hope you'll stay with me at the Oxford tonight, then."

"Thanks for the invite, Jeff. But I'd better stay close to home for the time being." Luke supplied a short version of Matt's diagnosis and his unexpected stay in Denver for treatment. "So, despite my summer hours, I can't be as available as I was. But I'm sure you're busy with meetings and board protocols and whatever."

"Denver won't be the same without your company."

"You mean, without my ass?"

"Man, what's the matter?"

"Nothing, for you. With an ass in every port." Luke hesitated, wondering if he should stanch his anger before he went on. Count to ten? Naw. "Anyway, what's she like, Jeff? I'll bet she's great. Smart, pretty, compliant. A country girl. A great mom, too. Did you meet her in the Ag program at CSU?"

Jeff's beer arrived, which gave him something to do during the silence that followed. He traced a curlicue in the mug's frost and sighed. "She's not so compliant." When Luke remained silent, Jeff traced a curlicue in the other direction. "She spent summers at her grandmother's, not too far from your friend Emily's place, out in Congress Park."

"Ah, sweet old east Denver." Luke took another deep swig. "Just think, she and I breathed the same smog when we were little. Paddled through the same snot and piss in the kiddie pool at Congress Park. But nothing pure and rarified, nothing like the wholesome ranch life of your little boys."

Jeff studied his beer, carving more curlicues. "She was in environmental science at CSU. Ironic, huh?"

"So ironic I forgot to laugh! How conflicted she must feel about the family's cattle biz. The natural enemy of our environment. Hooves trample the creek bed, then transporting and chilling all that meat burns more carbon than anything while their methane farts warm the climate, and she—the poor nameless creature—"

"Cassie."

"Cassie, of course! Short for Cassandra, cursed to remain a virgin. But you wouldn't think a modern girl would be naïve about us homosexuals and whatnot. Hell, visiting granny, she probably heard all about my own disgraceful reputation."

"She's, like, ten years older than you."

"Of course, it's easy to deceive even wise middle-aged people when they're in love with you. Even us sophisticated Denverites believe what we want to believe. I myself, for example. I nurtured my delusion that you were such a wonderful guy."

"I'm sorry, Luke. I—"

"I'm sorry for Cassie. I'm sorry for your boys."

"Those boys—"

"Your lagoon of pure bullshit contaminates your property. Cassie and the boys have to live with the stench." Luke stood and stuck a wad of dollar bills under his emptied mug. "I hope nobody recognized you here with your secret boyfriend, like your in-laws or Cassie's old pool mates or your boys' uncles and aunts and cousins. Hide in your disguise and enjoy your beer, Mr. Douglas. *Auf wiedersehen. Adios.* Goodbye."

❖

July 22

Matt and I had a late evening chat on the patio. As sometimes happens, whether because he's just naturally sympathetic to everybody or just an opposite brat, Matt asked me to see things from Jeff's point of view. I didn't really want to. I wanted to wallow in his sympathy. Matt asked me to consider what it must be like to be a gay cattleman in some remote corner of Wyoming, to be the scion of an old, rich ranching family stuck in a fake marriage. Matt acknowledged I had a right to my righteous anger, but also implied I was being very *conventional* in my moral outrage. "Besides," he said, "you don't know if he really is in love with you. He might be, and he's tortured about that, too. Sometimes love has to find its own course, like a surging river. At flood stage, the established banks have to get obliterated."

"Great," I said. "Bad riverine poetry, just what I needed."

Luckily he was tired and had to get to sleep for his morning appointment under the new mask and his first zap of radiation. He'd spent most of the day in Ted'n'Kathy's home office, calling, emailing, or video conferencing with the shop in Fruita, reassuring Jenn in Pittsburgh ("It's actually great, in a way. The treatments are gonna cure my lousy balance"), rearranging canoe trips for clients, and dealing with vendors.

After that foodless lunch with Jeff, I spent the day doing the opposite, ignoring all calls and messages. I studied ethical philosophers like Kant and Singer in the shade of our pear and plum trees. At one point, I was distracted by the thought of Cassie Douglas visiting Denver, imagining her as a little kid running under the fragrant linden trees in Congress Park on her way to the playground. Ten years later, I would follow in her footsteps, inhaling that heady scent under those same branches, goofing around on the same slide and swing set. I might've run into her grandparents at King Soopers or after Mass. Cassie and I were both just know-nothing little kids sharing the same sidewalks, minding our own business, hoping for the best, but somehow as adults we got seduced by the same cowboy, screwed by the same lying prick.

❖

After a breakfast of corn flakes and strawberries, Matt insisted he could walk all by himself to the radiation oncology complex. "It's just for the mask fitting and my first brain zapping. You don't need to hold my hand. Stay home and get your homework done."

But Luke said he wanted to stretch his legs and joked that he could help save those poor marigolds and other helpless parkway plantings Matt would trample. It was beautiful, the deep blue Colorado summer sky still cool and merciful, arching cloudless over the midmorning. "Let's take Twelfth Avenue through the park," Luke said, thinking of the smoother, newer concrete footpaths crisscrossing Cheesman.

When they reached the park, the sprinklers' artificial dew still glistened on the meadows and evergreens. "It's gorgeous today," Matt said. "I was thinking how Dad, growing up in our house, footsteps from Botanic Gardens, became a biologist. And you, growing up footsteps from the cruising fields of Cheesman Park, grew up to be a big homo."

"What about you? Are you a closet queer or a closet biologist?"

"Luke, somebody in our little family had to be normal. That's my burden. Closet normal guy."

"Ha! You wear it on your sleeve, Mr. Normal. The only thing that ever surprised me about you was that you didn't join a fraternity at Boulder."

"Come on. I'm an asshole, sure, but not that much of an asshole."

Twelfth Avenue delivered them on its smooth curve right to Franklin Street, a straight shot to the stoplight for crossing Colfax, then four blocks north to Radiation between the new and demolished hospitals. "Whoa, there, Mr. Normal!" When they walked an ancient flagstone sidewalk on Franklin, Matt stumbled on his own feet, pirouetting into somebody's little parkway garden of peonies and periwinkle. Luke helped retrieve him, pulling him back by the arm. "We've got to remember that you need to stay right of me. That way, when you veer off, you'll bump into me rather than become a menace to Denver's private gardens. And public order."

"No biggie. Those peonies are already down for the season, and besides, you're not going to walk with me to the hospital from here on out. You're not invited."

"I think I just proved how indispensable I am, invited or not."

Matt continued to stumble on the old, uneven flagstone walkways and continued to veer right toward innocent plantings on the smoother concrete. Otherwise, he would drag his left foot as if it had gone to sleep. Listening to Matt's litany of shop chores he would need to manage long distance,

Luke switched to his brother's right, enduring Matt's random collisions all the way to Radiation.

❖

July 23

Matt seemed unable to fully concentrate before this morning's radiation appointment. A nurse took us into a conference room and inquired about his advance directive, which he had already completed before he kayaked Class 5 rapids on a river in Peru, and laid down the law about sun protection for his head and neck during treatment. Matt did zero in, though, when she prohibited alcohol and marijuana. Even just one beer or one doobie? he'd asked, incredulous, prompting the nurse to hold forth about how fragile his gray matter would become. The nurse got even more serious. With both the tumor itself and the radiation doses, think of the stress your poor brain is going to be under.

❖

July 24

I'm writing this late on the patio, enjoying a nip of cold white wine before bed. I've been reading more Leo Strauss when I should be trying to craft a draft out of my pages of notes on ethics theories applied to the Summitville disaster, but it's easier to keep reading and spinning out an ever more complex web of rough notes. I have a mandatory meeting with

Grumpy later this week, and I feel like I have almost nothing new for him to revile and reject.

Meanwhile I've been busy ignoring Jeff's calls. As for his emails, I delete them all without opening, trying my best to ignore the subject lines.

Matt hit the sack earlier, lying fully dressed and open-doored on his old single bed, Toonces curled up at his stocking feet. His evening Frisbee session must've zonked him out. He invited me along but I made excuses, so he jogged, which he claims is easier and steadier than walking, over to Emily's to collect her and Marco and on to City Park. Gail decided to join them, so they formed a happy pack of joggers and tossed Frisbees without me.

Matt didn't mention anything when he got back, but I imagine Emily filled him in on Marco's ongoing ostracism of the Disgusting Fag Brother. I'm sure Gail and Marco were over the moon about a surprise visit by the charismatic, normal Devlin brother they all missed so much. Did they wonder what he was doing in Denver on a weeknight? I don't know what he or Emily told them. Was I jealous of their stupid Frisbee Family Fun in the park? Hell yes.

I've got to get more exercise myself (187.5 lbs). At noon, I rode my bike to Congress Pool for a pretty weak lap swimming session, stopping after a plodding kilometer. When I dried off on the deck, I felt hollowed out under the hallucinatory July sun, imagining the doses of radiation I was receiving by just being a nearly naked, exposed earthling. I was glad when the wailing hordes of daycare kids gave me an excuse to get up and go. Matt was still snoozing on the downstairs couch when I got back. After thunderclouds cooled off the late afternoon, I worked in the garden, stirring the unruly compost pile, attacking weeds, deadheading Mom's petunias and geraniums, and pulling out the brown spears of the spent iris and spring bulbs, a kind of midsummer postmortem.

This morning's was only the second of Matt's treatments, but it already feels like a routine. I let myself into his room after I heard his alarm, and while I insisted on joining him on his way to treatments and back, he got dressed and he fought his way into his khaki shorts, missing the leg hole and his balance and almost falling. He cursed the shorts as if they were the problem, then confessed he'd been fighting like that with getting his pants and boxers off and on for the last several months. I had to remind him to wear a cap and cover his bare neck for our walk across the park and up Franklin. He borrowed my red Boy Scout scarf and powder blue KUVO cap and looked ridiculous.

On our walk, he described the basic treatment routine. They take him through double doors and a lead curtain into a large lab where he lies on a moveable table with his feet raised. They strap on a yellow and blue mesh mask he says looks like Homer Simpson's big head, snapping it in place like an air filter and making sure there's not a millimeter of wiggle room. They warn him to stay still as possible. Then the technicians get the hell out of the treatment room while a massive machine emits red and green beams for about ten or fifteen minutes. He peeked, though they implored him to shut his eyes throughout. When the beams stop, the technicians return from a control room and move the table.

When Dr. Nilsson met with us after the treatment, Matt immediately asked about the beer ban. Nilsson dismissed the nurse's prohibition and even broke his shy character to raise an imaginary glass and say, "Live it up!" Either indulging Matt or overcome with pity or both, he touched the back of Matt's skull tenderly and asked it how it was going. He stressed Matt could call off the treatments if they ever became overwhelming. Matt continued to claim he was headache free and except for the balancing problem, all was even better than normal, especially now that he could still enjoy a beer or twelve. Of the first brain zappings, he reported he was glad that was over. "Oh, it's just beginning," Nilsson told him.

❖

Out on the patio after Luke and Matt demolished a king-sized veggie take 'n' bake pizza, Matt tried out an eye ointment for his right eye, which had been drying out. Over cold light beers, they debated disclosure. Luke wanted to contact their parents through the research sponsors' emergency contacts in Denver and Quito. Raising his beer and a gnawed remnant of pizza crust, Matt proclaimed, "Look at me. Does this look like an emergency?"

"Yes. Your eye looks like shit, all red and puffy. Why do you keep minimizing this? When you call Jenn, I've heard you make it sound like the radiation is some kind of miracle cure."

"But it feels like that to me. Honest, Luke."

"Anyway, Ted'n'Kathy'll kill us if we leave them in the dark about your tumor and the treatments."

"It's a family tradition. Remember Mom's scare with breast cancer that turned out to be misdiagnosed? Or Ted's shoulder surgery that went so well but was a lot riskier than he ever let on. When we were away at school, aren't you glad they didn't tell us until it was all over and everything was fine? What would've been the point?"

"That's not the point. And I didn't like not knowing until afterward. No chance to cheer them up or bring Mom flowers."

Matt waved a hand to indicate Kathy's flower beds. "She likes living ones."

"We still don't know how your situation is going to turn out, and they deserve to be kept informed."

"It's not a question of deserving. They're our parents. They deserve anything and everything. I want them to be happy about the engagement and bask in that. But why distract them from their research over these stupid treatments? They'll just worry."

"They should worry, Matt! This is freaking serious."

"But why not let 'em know when I'm doing even better, once the radiation really kicks in? And even after three doses, I already feel so much better! I almost feel like the radiation is giving me more energy and knocking out those headaches." Matt blatantly changed the subject to his plans to expand his shop's inventory and repair capacity when he got back to Fruita, and his hopes to add cross-country guided ski tours, plus yurt to yurt adventures to his winter weekends. "Remember the first time Mom and Dad took us to the Never Summer yurts up in the Bighorns? How much we freaked out when we realized they weren't behind us anymore?"

"Yeah, when we were skiing between Ruby Jewel and North Canadian."

"We thought they were lost somewhere in the lodgepole pines or marshes forever."

Luke, of course, remembered it well. After waiting what seemed like a half hour, the brothers had dropped their packs beside the twisting trail and hustled back along the deep snow tracks through a stand of pines and herringboned back up a ridge, probably a Jeep trail in the warm season, to save their folks from whatever menace they'd encountered. At the top, they found Ted'n'Kathy leaning on their poles, taking in the vista of North Park and the snow-serrated Sierra Madre range off west, cooing and smooching. At eleven and nine, Matt and Luke stopped herringboning and shared the same relief, then disgust. "Yuck."

❖

July 26

Back on the patio. Late. Can't really sleep while Matt snores in the deep slumber of innocents and fools in his room. His door open when I passed just now, he was still dressed in a T-shirt (mine) and shorts (mine), his bed lamp still on, the fan whirring in the window, his phone mashed on the pillow, and Toonces' muzzle mashed in the crook of his knees.

He called Jenn in Pittsburgh tonight, bringing her and me up to date. With no treatments scheduled on weekends, Matt's planning to drive back to Fruita with her when she flies into Denver Friday night so he can pack some clothes of his own for the duration. He also plans to put in some hours at the shop, where his two-man, one-girl staff is going frantic without him. He assured me Jenn is going to drive both ways, as she plans to come back with him Sunday night and stay here with him for as long as she can. The Pennsylvania commercial work forced her to drop her summer acting class and her hopes for a role in the Chekov play festival.

Matt and Jenn are planning a simple wedding after Matt's course of treatment, maybe late August or Labor Day weekend. Sitting right here beside me, phone to his good ear, staring out at Kathy's flowers in the twilight, Matt told Jenn that his grandparents, Ted's folks, got married in the Botanic Gardens while Ted'n'Kathy took their vows right here in the Devlin family garden. Matt told me Jenn's response to that: "How sweet, how homey, but what about my folks' yard in Grand Junction?"

After he finished the call, Matt told me she was probably afraid of hurting her folks' feelings. Plus, Grand Junction people can't stand it when Denver always gets all the glory. But her folks' place was a double-wide dropped on a dry acre outside Clifton with a view of a trailer park across a dry, gulley—brown lawn, bare earth, and a dead cottonwood.

"Sounds like they conserve water well," I told him. "True Coloradans."

"They're more like hillbillies."

"At least they're sustainable hillbillies," I said, "and it's the vows that count, not the venue."

Researching earlier today, I was half trying to see if I can apply much Sartre to historical ethics pertinent to Summitville, in hopes of impressing Grumpy in a draft section of my thesis I'm sending him. I wasn't getting anywhere thumbing through *Being and Nothingness*, but now thoughts of Matt and Jenn's wedding help me understand Sartre's point about existence preceding essence, the very eponymous heart of existentialism's meaning.

It's so refreshing they aren't going to try to put on the Great American Wedding Show but instead want to get hitched in a backyard, hillbilly or not. It means they don't view a wedding as having a pre-existing essence like so many couples, all the pile of must-haves and must-dos and the weird little customs and traditions and all the tension and ill feeling they can generate. It means they're starting off making their own meaning as they go, not trying to fit their marriage into some prefab, ill-sized rubber room of convention. Existence before essence, flexibility over fixed truths. I got it!

And speaking of conventional thinking, my old Cath-o-lick pal Emily stopped by to pick me and Matt up for a walk to the park after dinner. Marco, she said, decided to stay home with Gail, "helping out with tons and tons of house chores," so the three of us did a lap around Cheesman. I tried subtly as possible to make sure Matt kept between us so I could steady him if I needed to, but the jogging path was wide and fairly empty and Matt's gait was less leftward-leaning, so it wasn't much of a problem.

When we ended up in front of the Pavilion to feel the breeze licking the fountains and watch the sunset over the Rockies, Emily started in on this line of questioning I could tell she'd been saving up.

"How long are you going to keep it from everyone, and are we supposed to be your enablers in the big secret of the closet brain tumor? It was interesting watching you play Frisbee the other night.

Odd that the Graceful One was tossing it so clumsily
and missing it so often. And Marco sure noticed," she
said. "Gail wanted to know if you'd had too many
beers. When do I get to tell my mom and son what
their beloved friend is going through?"

"Beloved friend? Come on, Em, that's laying it
on a little thick."

"What should I call you, then? Surrogate co-
father and son? How about secretive creep?"

"Look, Marco and Gail mean the world to me.
That's why I don't want to worry them until I get
better." Matt rubbed his forehead.

Emily shot a look at me behind Matt's back. She
had to protect my big secret during our schooldays
and clearly didn't enjoy putting on a similar show
again now that we were what passed for adults. But
worse, I could read her disbelief that getting better
was just a matter of laser-sharp beams of radioactivity
plus time, and that Truth was, of course, fixed and
eternal.

❖

Matt bustled around Friday morning after his last treatment of the week, even making a giant spinach, mushroom,
and swiss omelet for breakfast on return from radiation.
Watching Matt crash in the passenger seat when they drove
to the airport to pick up Jenn at noon, Luke worried about the
long drive the couple planned to take to Grand Junction that
afternoon.

But when he saw the relief in Jenn's face and how much
their reunion blissed both of them out, Luke relaxed and
changed his mind. A long weekend at the condo in Fruita

might be exactly what they both needed. Jenn would be freed from the tensions of sudden commercial stardom and the pressure to replicate in Pennsylvania everything that had charmed Colorado. Matt could escape from the relentless radiation schedule and the fatigue-stricken days of empty time, unwanted leisure under the stress of running a business without being on-site. For a couple days, at least, he could be back with his staff, up to his elbows in bicycle grease.

Luke saw them off from the front porch, wheeling away in Matt's white van with its hippie-style lettering and flower power doodles of mountain bikes with daisies for tires, *Book Cliff Cyclery and Horsethief Adventures.* For the first time all summer, Luke felt the cold pressure of empty time himself. Almost without meaning to, he found himself wandering his mother's Old Lady Garden, plucking a weed here and there and deadheading blossoms in a flourishing section of the backyard that surrounded a bench and a small flagstone patio. Kathy Devlin devoted these flower beds to old-fashioned flowers she remembered from her grandmother's garden: feral stalky stuff like hollyhocks, larkspur, cosmos, and all those tall, lurid pink phlox popping up in prolific abandon.

He heard Judith's low, growly voice and saw her waving over the hollyhocks. Her elfin, red-nosed face appeared in an opening between the budding vines rampant on the collapsing fence between the yards. After she interrogated Luke about Matt and Jenn, out of the blue she asked, "How is Thoreau going, Luke?"

"Disappointing, tell you the truth. Lots of *Walden* seems grouchy and dull."

"Yep. Even though he died young, he was a terrible old crank."

"Why didn't you tell us that in junior English?"

"I put a brave face on it because he was in the curriculum,

and I had no choice. Plus, I didn't want to disillusion your innocent childish minds."

"Since when?"

"Only *Civil Disobedience* and that 'War of the Ants' thing are worth the trouble. Meanwhile, he's really a phony and *Walden* is the worst classic in the canon. Pretending to live in the wilderness alone when he was strolling the short path to his mother's for meals. Footsteps from his shack on the pond, he'd go begging and bitching at the Emersons' table. Bah!"

It could have been horrible for Luke and Matt to have their high school English teacher right next door, but it turned out to be kind of wonderful. Because Judith was kind of wonderful. They'd consult her over the fence, and instead of exchanging cups of sugar, she'd advise the family on good reads, commas after relative clauses, iambic pentameter, and especially footnotes. She was also politically attuned in a way the distracted Devlins weren't, so Ted'n'Kathy valued her advice on candidates for state office or loopy, deceptive ballot proposals, and they could always count on her to have good liquor in stock for social emergencies.

When Matt was about six, after Judith went through a divorce, he wondered why she was alone on holidays and invited her to Thanksgiving. After that, her bean casserole became a family tradition on every holiday table. Judith would appear, frazzled from casserole fussing, already tipsy, passing flowers to Kathy and a bottle of wine from someplace deep in Romania or ex-Yugoslavia.

Relieved as a schoolboy dismissed to recess, Luke felt he had official permission to give up on *Walden*. He filled the rest of the day managing the little hassles of house-sitting, the recurring chores from feeding Toonces to watering the houseplants, sweeping the deck and porch, then remembering to feed himself.

❖

July 29

It's Sunday evening and I swear I heard the first clickety throb of crickets before it went silent, the inarguable overture of late summer, like they're tuning up to beckon us back to school. It's still so warm I'm tempted to push Toonces off my lap. I'm irritated by the extra thermal units this fat old hairball of a cat generates. Still, it's refreshing to mash a cold beer bottle against the side of my face and even better to sip it while I confront the blank page of this journal.

It feels challenging because I feel stuck now, half of me just wanting to lick my wounds over the sickening crash-and-burn of my hopeful little affair with Jeff, the other half humming with nonstop anxiety about Matt. I'm glad he has time to catch up with Jenn and his bike shop crew, but I'm worried about how draining the eight-hour round trip to Fruita in one short weekend might be. I just hope he keeps feeling energized and positive about the treatments next week, and that the prospect of the tumor metastasizing keeps receding like Nilsson's delicate blond hairline.

Another dateless Saturday night, the reality of being single again, Jeffless and resourceless, settled in. Damien stopped by after his shift, still in his scrubbies, to order me to meet him at Aunt Pete's for a cocktail with Dave Hunter, a gay English teacher everybody thinks I should pair up with. I appreciate

Damien's solicitude and amorous energy, but I don't have the heart to tell him I can't stand Dave Hunter.

As much as I tend to like English majors, Dave has just a touch enough of the fussy Mississippi sissy to put me off. I can't really tell Damien I mostly like masculine guys because Damien himself has never been the most butch homo on the block. Anyway, Damien changed into the extra club clothes he still keeps in his old room—now the guest room again—and insisted I needed a break from my own damn lugubrious self. So at eleven we walked down to Colfax, where I tried to enjoy a cocktail on Aunt Pete's deck, and tried to be game, semi-intelligent, and original by coaxing Dave into a conversation about Sartre. But he'd only seen the play *No Exit* and wasn't encouraged to read more of that kind of "bleak, godless French theorizing." Damien put in that my favorite novel was Sartre's *Nausea* and told Dave, "it's the perfect title, too. One big depressing puke."

All righty then. When Damien and Dave decided to head down to Damien's beloved cha-cha palace, I claimed fatigue and waved them on without me. Alone on the deck at Aunt Pete's, I tried my best to feel absorbed by the Saturday night fun/desperate vibe, but finished my drink standing stiffly at the bar, feeling numbed and aloof.

Walking home, the pressure of this solitude chilled the warm, starry night. I could make out the Big Dipper and Summer Triangle through the city's blazing night sky and could not stop myself from considering how cartoonish we humans are, putting familiar shapes on unconnected balls of galactic gas to comfort ourselves in a universe of pure random nothingness. I came home to this big empty house, with even Toonces hiding out somewhere, and felt the hollow distance of my family, Fruita seeming as remote as the Ecuadorian Amazon. But nothing felt as remote as another chance for love.

❖

Monday evening, right after she got off work, Emily stopped by on her evening walk to see Matt and Jenn, but they had gone grocery shopping. Jenn wanted to make a summery dinner for the brothers—pesto on focaccia bread, green and fruit salads. Luke and Emily strolled to Cheesman to soak up the evening breeze. "I was so glad to see Jenn and Matt pull up last evening," Luke told Emily, "I almost threw rice from the front steps."

"It's kind of premature for that, Luke. They haven't even chosen a date, right? Anyway, it's not like you to feel creeped out when you're alone. Your true self is an antisocial hermit, happy in your scholarly solitude."

"I guess I've changed. I could use more scholarliness but less solitude. I got used to Matt knocking around the house last week. It reminds me of when I was still a preschooler and used to yearn for him to come home from first grade. I'd sit on the front steps, keeping an eye down the block for the first sight of my big brother."

"What a memory you have. I try not to remember anything before I turned twenty-five."

"It's going to be different now, too, with Jenn joining Matt for his morning dose of radioactivity. I'm going to miss seeing my Male Waiting Room ladies."

"I'm sure they're going to miss you—" Emily cut herself off, startled by a volleyball player calling her name and yelling that the team missed her. She laughed and jogged across the lawn, accepting the applause of the team she'd played on last summer with an elaborate bow. The informal team was mostly friends of Emily's and Luke's from high school, whose captain told Emily, "We'll even take Luke if we can have you back." Emily had been a star. Luke had been barely semi-adequate, and the alumni would not weep if this evening's opponent, a group from Aunt Pete's, drafted him out of gay solidarity and human mercy.

"Maybe we'll come back for the September tourney," Emily told the alumni team, waving off as she and Luke continued through the central meadow. "Maybe we should've joined the team this summer," she said.

"Don't look at me. I didn't have a fan club imploring me to come back."

"I think I wanted to work late and rack up those extra commissions, but I don't feel like I've gained an extra minute of freedom. Or any extra commissions."

"And I was supposed to finish my thesis with the freedom I've had. But I've hardly got my ideas formed. What happened?"

"Summer, beautiful but stupid," Emily said. "Winter never goes by like this."

"I'm surveying my philosophical sources to support the idea that inaction is a form of evil. In which case, when it comes to my thesis, I'm pretty evil."

"Or just ineffective. Sounds like you have been researching, just not getting where you expected to be."

"That's even more depressing."

"At least you won't go to hell for blissing out under your plum tree, smoking pot and not doing squat."

"This is a ridiculous conversation. In the eyes of the random universe—"

"Which must be blind, therefore eyeless—"

"We're like little bugs scuttling around from leaf to leaf. Imagine what we'd think, how we'd laugh, if we heard those bugs taking nuanced positions on evil and inaction in a universe they think is the size of this park and still incomprehensible. Just sayin'."

"I didn't hear either of us say anything very nuanced, Luke. And who says we deserve to be compared to bugs? Maybe we're the microscopic germs living on the bugs in your analogy, or even the germs of germs." As they reached the playground, she traced a square in a bare patch with the heel of her sneaker. "Imagine the almost infinite number of germs' germs living in this square of earth. Which they think is so vast, they're unable to comprehend the park, let alone the surrounding city, let alone the surrounding continent or planet. Etcetera."

"Thanks, Catholic Chick. You're making my point."

"And you're missing mine, Existential Punk. Those of us who respect the infinite understand we are no more than those germs' germs in the eyes of God, who is blessed with perfect vision. We are as obscure and unable to understand our place in creation or the nature of the Creator as those germs. Yet we keep speculating on our tiny section of our playground dirt as if it were even worth mentioning in the infinitude of God's immensity. Just sayin'."

AUGUST

August 1

Emily and I had a new variant on the Conversation last evening when we walked around Cheesman. We've been debating this subject for going on fifteen years, at least, since I left the Church. It doesn't ever really start or finish, like a pickup game in some eternal public basketball court. But I've got to admit that her stirring in the analogy of our infinitesimally feeble understanding really shut me up. Emily was right yesterday evening. I didn't expect that to be her point, that our potential for understanding God is impossible, attempted only by arrogant, atheistic germs such as me. It's a useful metaphor, one that's eluded me all these years: The unknowable essence of God is exactly *why* we have faith. The vastness of the god being or creative force remains beyond our capabilities.

Sweet baby Jesus, it's already August. Despite my efforts to slow the quick wink of summer by keeping a record, I feel I've squandered it, both in meager enjoyment and meager thesis progress. (Though I did better today, a good mile of noontime laps at Congress pool—back to 186 lbs—and whole afternoon of diving into more research.) Another blink, and I'll be attending this year's teacher orientation, reorganizing my classroom, and writing lesson plans to get me through the first weeks of my new Early American History class.

Sunday and Monday's bleak self-drama was a good setup for today's prep for meeting with Grumpy this week. He wants to go over the draft chapters in person in his office, which I think is either a bad sign or nothing more than a signal he's a sadist and wants me to wonder and worry in advance of his inevitable disapproval.

I think I've got a solid section on the competing philosophical perspectives of Strauss & Singer, and now I may have found a way to bring in Sartre. It lies in the corporate negligence and abandonment of Summitville and Sartre's view that evil lies in shirking responsibility, indifference, in not acting.

Jenn & Matt are calling me to BBQ. Grilled veggies and tofu dogs. Though I'm not crazy about the reason for this unexpected company, this newly formed family, I'm enjoying their presence in the house. Nothing like the anticipation of being tormented by my big brother and future sister-in-law to pull my head out of Summitville. Really, I feel like a kid again, just digging this deepening attachment to people I love.

❖

The next day while Jenn and Luke were finishing a noon salad on the patio, Matt struggled to swallow his greens. "This just happens, out of the blue," he said, gulping and gasping for breath. "'Scuse me. I've got to remember to cut things into smaller pieces."

He had been emailing his shop and waiting for a response between mouthfuls, but now Ted and Kathy popped on his tablet screen for a video chat.

"We came into Tena on a supply run and look at this, there might even be a spell of steady electricity and internet service!" Kathy said, laughing.

"You look great, Mom," Matt said. "God, I'm so glad to see your smile. I worry, you know, you'll drift away on some random log in the Amazon deeps."

"Don't worry, son," Ted said, squeezing his face on screen beside Kathy's. "We usually get around by regulation motorboat, not random logs."

"Doesn't matter, Dad. You could stand up, get excited by some rare water lily or bug, and there you go, kerplunk headfirst into the great river. Piranha food."

"We don't have piranha in this part of the watershed—" Kathy said.

"We're on a pretty puny tributary," Ted put in.

"And your father does almost all of his rare butterfly research on land, so no need to worry. I'm sticking to the flowers, like Ferdinand the Bull. I don't know anything about bugs anyway, and he's completely ignorant of my rare blossoms."

"I beg your pardon," Ted said. "I know a lot more than the average bull."

Jenn laughed at this, which inspired a moment of dislocation. "Jennifer, is that you? Where are you two?" Kathy asked. "Matt, aren't you at the shop?"

"No, we've having lunch," Jenn said, exchanging a cautionary look with Matt. As if imitating Ted'n'Kathy, they put their heads together to block any view of the house and patio.

"Oh, Jenn! How wonderful to see your face. I have to say I've been spending a lot of time daydreaming about the wedding. I never thought I would become one of those gushy mothers, but I just can't help looking forward to it."

"We just need to know when you and Dad can get back home."

"You give us a date, and we'll get home in plenty of time to help with the wedding," Kathy said. "I can't wait! If you can't get the Botanic Gardens, we'll be happy with the backyard."

"Or, more likely," Matt hastened to put in, "Jenn's folks' yard in Grand Junction."

"Of course," Kathy said. "Sorry. I forgot that Jenn's family is there in Junction. Denver chauvinism, you know. Well, it'll be lovely. The Monument! The Mesa! Maybe we can all tour the vineyards in Palisade after the festivities."

"Yeah, we'll have a blast, Kathy," Jenn said.

"Besides, don't forget who's been taking care of your garden." Matt added, "In Denver, I mean."

"How is Luke doing?" Ted asked. "Have you talked to him recently?"

"Great, Dad, I'm right here!" Luke said, ignoring Matt's slicing-finger-to-your-throat gesture. "And the yard looks so good tourists are wandering over from the Botanic Gardens, thinking it's an annex. If Matt will get his claws off the tablet, I'll give you a panorama."

"So you're all in Denver now, not Fruita?" Kathy asked. "What's going on?"

"Jenn just got in from Pennsylvania. You know those commercials I mentioned in my emails?"

"Yeah, the clean energy series?" Ted said. "Very exciting, Jenn!"

"Well, I picked her up at DIA, and I'm taking her back to Grand Junction on Friday. So we're spending a little family time with Lukie."

"I'd give anything to be there with you. Tell me, am I being an idiot for daydreaming about being a grandmother?"

"Who can blame you?" Jenn asked. "Matt and I want to start a family as soon as we've established a household. And maybe saved a few pennies."

"Imagine," Ted said, "a wedding, and *then* children. It's so old fashioned, it's revolutionary."

They promised to firm up dates for the wedding, but Ted warned them they might have a more difficult time than usual exchanging emails or having chats. "We're going even deeper into the preserve. Exchanging motorboats for canoes. It's our last chance before the bulldozers start chewing it up."

"We should emerge for a little time in Tena in two weeks or so," Kathy said. "Whatever dates you decide, we'll book our tickets out of Quito then."

Luke managed to grab Toonces where he'd prowled during the video chat, front paws on the back door screen. He filled the chat screen with the cat's fat face and shook his paw goodbye as Ted and Kathy vanished, waving back and blowing kisses.

"Geez, Luke, what did you speak up for?" Matt asked. "It would've been so much easier if they just kept believing we were in Fruita."

"Oh, I was supposed to pretend like I wasn't here? Along with pretending that you're not undergoing radiation therapy for the world's largest known fucking brain tumor?"

"Pretending's not hurting anyone. You know what we agreed."

"And I didn't break the agreement. I didn't say a thing."

"They're going to find out soon enough, just when I'm

done with treatments, okay? Meanwhile, help us pick a date in September or October for the wedding."

"They're going to be pissed," Jenn said to Matt, placing her hand gently on his back, "that you kept them in the dark about this. Along with finding out what my 'clean energy series' really is. Especially after they've spent months trying to save the Amazon from the ravages of dirty energy."

❖

August 3

Realizing I haven't been outdoors very much since my canoe trip with Matt last month, and with Jenn taking Matt to treatments, I got up early and headed up to Indian Peaks for a solo hike up South Arapahoe Peak. I knew it wasn't exactly kosher to go solo up a summit, but this trail is usually a traffic jam of hikers, so I figured I would hardly be alone.

After the bumpy road up to the Fourth of July trailhead above Eldora and the immediate, steep hike through wild gardens clotted with wildflowers, the pinks, blues, and whites of larkspur, monkshood, penstemon, columbine, cow parsnip, parrot beak, and baby elephant head competing in profusion with neighboring yellows—wild yarrow, sunflowers, buttercup, and nameless yellow composites, I mean everywhere. I've always loved how this first segment of the trail astonishes newcomers with so many pleasures and varieties of growth in so few footsteps.

Then the Mount Neva massif, the waterfall across the valley, the dramatic, re-vegetating old avalanche chutes—they still flabbergast me, and

I've been hiking this trail since I was a baby in a papoose bundle being traded back 'n' forth between Ted'n'Kathy. Not to mention it was a pluperfect morning, deep blue cloudless skies at least twenty degrees cooler than Denver's swampy midsummer haze. It was also amazingly quiet once I passed the Diamond Lake cutoff. By the time I reached the ghost mine and the trail junction for the Arapahoe peaks, I couldn't see another soul anywhere above timberline, amazing for early August.

All by myself, I was starting to feel a little desolate about that sonofabitch Jeff. It just came over me, probably because I'd planned to take him hiking here, but our affair ended before summer did.

A cloud passed overhead, its sudden chill welcome, but it had plenty of company massing in the west over Neva, just opposite. It was still well before eleven, and I hoped to make it to the summit for lunch by around one, then beat the inevitable afternoon thunderclouds and get back to the trailhead dry and happy. Ahead of me, a party of three climbers started up the switchbacks at the very beginning of the tundra. It was reassuring to know they'd be on the summit when I got there, and though what came next was very stupid, it seemed rational, cautious, and well thought out as I started up the peak.

Even though it was still sunny enough to feel the heat on my bare neck and arms, a few drops of rain from stray clouds kept spritzing the trail, then bigger drops that plopped on the top of my head, but all comically sparse in the disco ball scatter of sunlight. When I was halfway up the switchbacks, sudden winds shoved the little clouds into bigger combinations, which started pelting hail. Soon the sun was blotted out completely, and lightning struck down valley. I was up on the ridge, thinking it would all blow over by one o'clock and I'd have sunshine for my lunch on the summit. Great.

As I proceeded up the rocky, west-facing, exposed trail toward the peak, five separate little rainstorms pelted me and tormented me with nearby lightning strikes. I yanked my rain jacket out of my pack, which usually does the magic trick of making the storm pass away.

Not this time. When I reached the marmot town, a jumble of boulders where I usually stopped to hang out with the critters, I had to crouch under dripping rocks praying the lightning gods wouldn't choose my particular rock. When I finally scrambled to the top in a brief pause of sunshine, I found out the party of three must have aborted their climb, maybe glissading down the glacier to the south, because I was completely alone.

I prowled the summit ridge all by myself, too scared to be scared, watching the storms rising in Hiroshima clouds over Neva like some freaking out-of-control lightning machine. I couldn't do anything but watch the new storms attack the Arapahoe Peaks at warp speed until I was completely enfolded in blinding clouds. My windbreaker started making crackling noises I'd never heard before as if it was ready to explode or disintegrate.

I realized the crackling was the sound of my hair standing upright, full of static, against my rain hood. The hair on my arms did the same against my sleeves.

All I could do was drop face forward and crouch into yet another patch of rocks, offering my back to the lightning, which forked all over hell all around the summit. The rocks themselves were crackling now. The whole peak was alive with masochistic desire to be struck again and again.

Facedown in buzzing rocks like a hail-addled little rabbit, I had plenty of time to ponder how I'd always been blasé about lightning in the mountains. When friends warned me to be careful, I'd said, "Well, it wouldn't be such a bad way to go," or some other fatalistic hooey.

Now I realized it might be the worst way to go. Maybe the lightning didn't kill you all at once. Maybe it just disabled you with a paralyzing burn so you lay there, helpless, unable to move, your skin on fire, screaming for hours if not days until you finally expired in agony.

Instead, the last storm passed overhead, with nothing over Neva but blazing blue skies. The winds ceased, and steam rose everywhere on the rocky crest. Except for a few piles of fast-melting hail, there was blinding sun. The tantrum had moved east to torment Boulder and the far plains.

I sat on a flat, saturated rock and gulped down my sandwich, alone and bewildered. I wondered if Matt's daily dose of radiation ever felt to him like a lightning strike and its aftermath of stunned, slowly flatlining terror, and whether he was more affected than he let on. And like me now, grateful for my life.

❖

"For the first time, Mr. Devlin," Grumpy said, "I'm seeing promise here, a real scholarly series of guideposts and not a mere series of name-dropping gimmicks. Strauss does indeed match up well with the dangers of unchecked *laissez-faire* development at Summitville. Singer is also a good choice for a utilitarian analysis of the harm of the pollution catastrophe versus the intended monetary gains for the corporation. But adding Sartre, this idea of inaction as the great crime, the investors' lack of a lived-out moral choice, is where you have potential to merge ethics with history in an original way. What I need now, what I'm hoping you'll send me before mid-August, is the in-depth, chronological case study to flesh out these concepts."

Luke could barely do more than nod vigorously and haltingly agree to draft the case study ASAP. Apart from the usual condescension and blithe backhanded insults, there didn't seem to be a catch. Just a nearly impossible deadline.

Elated, he stopped by the department office to share the good results with Renata, the department manager, who laughed in open glee, crying, "At last, my Lucas!" in her perfect Germanic English. Then Luke ducked into the adjacent department library to check out a manual of research citation procedures. While he located the volume behind the half-open door, Luke could glimpse Grumpy emerging from his office to hand some papers to Renata.

"Sometimes, I hate to admit, we are too happy to hurry certain of our graduate students out of these hallowed hallways. It's actually offensive, isn't it, when the stereotype proves too true. The vaunted shallowness of a certain, shall we say, sexual minority? He oozes it."

Renata accepted the papers without a word and placed them precisely in a plastic tray. Luke watched her move the tray farther left and forward to the edge of her desk. She tapped her desktop computer's mouse so that the wallpaper changed from an array of her grandchildren's faces to a portrait of Einstein sticking out his tongue. American since her adolescence, seeming dumbstruck, Renata played the immigrant card. "The idioms, Professor, still bedevil me at times. *Oozing a sexual minority?*"

"No, no, my dear. Oozing shallowness."

"Oh. But the *sexual minority*? By that you mean the gay?"

"Ah, Renata, I can't say that. PC police, you know. But I'm charmed by your translation." Grumpy winked and returned to his darkling quarters.

❖

Aug 5

It's been a spooky Saturday, odd for high summer. I keep thinking of the concerned look on Jenn's face yesterday morning, just after their walk from Matt's radiation session before they took off for Fruita in the late morning. She teasing Matt gently about his shuffling, sideways shamble, then stopped herself. I sensed her acting skills more than her sincerity when she declared how great it was going to be to get back to the condo and start exploring their wedding options while Matt got things caught up at the shop.

Not really wanting to face the weekend alone, I waved them off from the front porch. A tight feeling in my gut had me wondering what the hell it portended besides too many of the blueberry pancakes Matt and I made for late breakfast. More likely, my stomach was churning with dread over this afternoon's appointment with Grumpy. After almost getting praise from him for my Sartre connection, I happened to overhear his smarmy, secretive dismissal of my stereotypical vaunted queer shallowness. At least now I have a better idea why he's always seemed to barely tolerate me, since it could hardly be for my bland, normative personality or my harmless son-of-professors deference to academia's pettiness. Or my middle-class politeness to pricks.

Anyway, spooky: Just after eleven this morning, an early storm started to kick in, darkening the sunny sky in an instant, a west wind shaking the silver maple branches overhead so the leaves thrashed their wild green and silver semaphore all up and down the block. Then a drama queen series of bursting rainstorms after noon, real gutter-washers that almost deserved the term *monsoon* the TV weather people like to overuse every time a stray summer storm douses our dry, godforsaken steppes.

In the cool of the storms' aftermath, I decided on a seven-mile run around Cheesman and down around Washington Park, dancing around the huge puddles in the jogging paths and sinking into the spongy trail along the Marion Parkway. I, or my endorphin rush, exulted in the leaf-breezy late afternoon and that oxymoronic joy of effortless exertion.

Damien surprised me after my shower, appearing downstairs in his scrubbies with Chinese takeout, bearing a carton of sesame tofu for me. We noshed on the patio, ingesting the evening's cool as much as the gooey calories and glorious cheap corporate lagers. We exchanged our lines for Inane Conversation #473, in which he argued for the necessity of our going out together to the cha-cha palace because:

1. it was Saturday night
2. and sure to be overflowing with Cute Guys,
3. plus, I, the decrepit Luke Devlin, would be Turning Thirty in a few short weeks and all our youthful beauty was going to be squandered and soon lost forever if we didn't get out on that dance floor at Tracks tonight.

Somehow I managed to beg off, maybe because I had the truth on my side. I really needed to work every remaining minute the rest of the weekend on reviewing as much Summitville research as I could. I think Damien was convinced by my account of Grumpy's arbitrary deadline because he backed off. Instead, he decided to head to his own place to begin the long work of prettying himself for the disco and braving it alone.

I worked past closing time, deep in the online weeds of pollution reports and legal accounts of the investors' negligence and inaction, some of them PDFs of handwritten notes from the 1980s deep inside folders of folders of legalistic evidence packets. The challenge hung over my yellow pad notes: how to organize a historical narrative that was more than chronological or even analytical, but shaped by my three philosophical tendencies. Around one thirty, I thought of Damien shutting down the cha-cha palace without me, hoping he found some wonderful Cute Guy to keep him company. I kept working past three in the morning with the dedication that detectives must feel, shifting details, ever on the cusp of solving a bloody crime.

❖

Luke made a big skillet of scrambled eggs Monday morning with Jenn chopping and sautéing the veggies, but they had to have them without Matt. He wanted to sleep as long as he could before his first radiation session of the week, so Jenn arranged with the technicians for a switch to early afternoon. "He pushed himself way too hard all weekend in Fruita, trying to catch up on paperwork and accounts at his shop and even joining the crew on repairs and tune-ups. He's such a bike geek, he can't stop himself from jumping in."

"He must be going nuts, not taking his after-work rides."

"Oh, he tried, Saturday evening. After it cooled off, he talked me into a quick spin out to the Cliffs to hit an easy trail…" Jenn deliberately steadied her breath. "Anyway, he was so frustrated because he had trouble throwing his right leg over the bike to get going, then wobbled a bit when he did. This is Matt! Struggling like he'd never hopped on a mountain bike before. He did all right once we got to the roads outside town, but we stopped at the first trailhead and didn't hit any trails at all. I could tell he was intimidated, freaked out by his unsteadiness, so I begged off at the trailhead, telling him it was starting to get too dark now, and that we ought to head back to town. He didn't argue, but the old Matt would've romped on those loop trails until the stars came out."

"Nice way to save his male pride."

Matt appeared in the kitchen doorway, bed-headed and puffy-eyed, looking rumpled in his T-shirt and boxers. Arms crossed, he leaned against the doorjamb. "Who's saving whose male pride?"

"I'm bolstering Luke's," Jenn said without missing a beat,

"to keep him cooking up these excellent veggie skillets." She rose to kiss him good morning. "We saved you some."

"Male pride or veggie skillets?" Matt pulled Jenn close, nuzzling her hair and nibbling her ear. "I'll just munch on these cute earlobes, thanks." He pointed to the back of his head. "Plus a side of ibuprofen, please."

❖

Aug 8

I invited Matt to join me on a bike ride after he got back from radiology. All I had to do was raise the seat on Dad's hybrid town bike to a height more suitable for a full-grown adult and check the air in the tires. But Matt was unexpectedly hesitant to come along, a first in the twenty-five years since the training wheels came off. He implied he wouldn't mind having them back and finally fessed up to having bouts of double vision. "It's a freaky feeling," he told me, "and it throws my balance off even more." That's what messed him up in Fruita. That's why he didn't want to try the single-track trails even though he knows them all by heart.

I wondered if it was caused by the treatments, but Matt said Nilsson told him double vision was a common symptom of brain stem tumors, and he was surprised Matt hadn't presented with it before now. He insisted I go for a ride myself and Jenn chimed in, claiming that she needed Matt to help her get ready for the BBQ they're planning for the evening.

With the thunderclouds cooling off the early

afternoon, I took off for the Cherry Creek bikeway and on to Confluence Park, then north on the Platte River trail, which I haven't done all season. I had an uneasy, queasy feeling as the air got heavier, an achy anxiety in my gut. The trees and shrubs lining the greenway had an August wiltedness, another reminder summer was slipping away and fast. The river itself was low enough that algae-caked shallows fingered the banks. Side channels cut off from the main flow, leaving ghostly, smelly mud behind. I decided to turn around at Riverside Cemetery. The ancient elms looked wintry in the heat, completely bare and long dead since the cemetery lost its water rights decades ago.

Riverside always makes me burn to teach Colorado history someday, if I could ever wrest it from the veteran teachers who keep clutching it close. I took a water break beside a pioneer grave so old the name had worn away, the limestone oxidized, erasing birth and death. Nearby, a massive angel's wingspan stretched over a marble vault. Next to it, stone dolomite cherubs guarded monuments bigger than servants' shacks, and thorny vines strangled the grave of a one-time newspaper king's concrete mausoleum.

Bare dirt and sand piled over humbler markers such as the one for the soldier Soule who refused to partake in the Indian genocide at Sand Creek in the 1860s, then was shot in the street after his return. Not far away was his commander, Chivington, who'd killed the women and children with gusto. Not far from Chivington was our territorial governor and university founder, John Evans, almost hidden in cheat-grass under flat stone plate. He'd dispatched Chivington to the killing field.

Back on the bike path, a brief thunder squall stirred dead twigs and heavy showers, sending a clutch of homeless men to gather under the shelter of cottonwoods. I joined them to wait out the rain. They all seemed newly expelled from life under roofs. Shooting the shit, they acted anxious to establish themselves with me as just guys, dudes who once rode the greenway too, just for laughs. I felt at home with them, ironically I guess, as this new anxiety chewed my innards, not in sync with anything else. I understood maybe too well their drive to declare their normality, their ownership of vanished property, their claim on anything: sobriety, diplomas, a floor, a ceiling, a front door, wife and kids, somebody to love.

❖

The BBQ was a typical Devlin backyard party, and its ordinariness cheered Luke after his ride to Riverside cemetery—a clutch of first cousins and their toddlers, a couple of Matt's old friends from high school and their wives, along with Damien, Emily, Gail, and, at last, Marco, who decided he could endure Luke's presence as a necessary evil in order to enjoy Matt's company.

As if by declaration, everyone decided to respond to Matt's changed condition with jokey good humor and optimism. Expansive plans accumulated for river expeditions and hikes so Matt could salvage the summer after his treatments ended and he was "back on his feet." The cousins crowded around Jenn and Matt to chat up the wedding, everyone planning to extend it to a vacation weekend on the Western Slope.

Luke took over grilling the hot dogs and burgers and their fake soy equivalents alongside the peppers and mushrooms Matt and Jenn had prepared. Gail appeared at his side, bearing beers for each of them. "So, should we be worried?" she asked Luke, her voice low. "Matt looks a bit worse for wear in the past week or so."

"We think it's because the dosage accumulates, but we don't really know. There'll be a conference with his radiology surgeon tomorrow."

"Emily says you guys still haven't notified Ted and Kathy."

"That's Matt's decision. He wants to fill them in after the treatments, so they don't worry while they're on the project."

"That sounds like a logical plan, but it's not a very good emotional one. Your folks are going to be royally pissed off, Luke. They'll want to know, not be protected from the truth. They're scientists, for the love of Pete."

"I couldn't agree more." Luke flipped over some burgers, nodding toward Matt, chatting now with Marco, who gestured with a Frisbee. "I wish you would take it up with him, Gail, because he won't listen to me on this subject."

Matt caught their gaze and moved closer to the grill, gently nudging Marco closer, too. "Hey, kid, I really can't play Frisbee right now. I've got to play host."

"Well, I'm a guest, right? So play with me."

"Okay, the truth is, I'm having this blurry, double vision thing going on. I don't want to embarrass myself too much by jumping after the Frisbee I think I see instead of the one you actually tossed. Luke, I'll take over grilling if you want to play with Marco."

"Great," Luke said, ready to hand over the spatula to Matt. "I'm kind of a Frisbee champion, if I do say so, Marco."

"It's okay," Marco said. "Never mind." He sliced the Frisbee across the yard, where it almost shaved a patch of pepper plants.

"Hey!" Gail said. "That's just plain rude, Marco. And careful where you throw that thing."

"I wanted to play with Matt, okay?"

"Well, I'm not sure I want to play with you, kid, if you're gonna flash so much attitude." Matt passed the spatula back to Luke, patting his shoulder. "You hurt my little brother's feelings."

"Like I've told you, Marco," Luke said, "I'm ready to be friends again whenever you are."

"I'm not ready."

"Then maybe I'm not ready to spend time with *you*," Matt said. "This is not cool, Marco. It'd be like rejecting me because I'm left-handed. I was born left-handed. I didn't have any choice."

Marco looked up at the three adults around the grill, holding his own. "It's different. Left-handed people still get married and have normal lives."

"So do gay people."

"With women, Matt," Marco said, "come on." As Emily joined the conclave around the grill, Marco ran off to retrieve the Frisbee from the slobbery mouth of a curious toddler.

"Where did he get this hardcore homophobia?" Matt asked. "Jeez."

"We can't control what he picks up from his uncles and cousins," Emily said, "on Carlos's side."

"He's gonna come around," Luke said. "I have faith."

"You, faith?" Emily said. "You have faith in nothing, Lucas Devlin."

Luke signaled around the crowded patio, using the spatula as a pointer. "Faith in humankind, my sister. Otherwise, why I am filled with love for my friends and family?"

Gail presented an empty bun on a paper plate for Luke to fill. "Because we are all so damn loveable."

❖

Aug 9

Thanks to Jenn saying she didn't want to get to Luke's big consult with Drs. Leibniz and Nilsson all sweaty, we drove the eight blocks. That helped convince Matt, since it was already hot and sultry by midmorning. But she's confided to me how exasperating it's been to walk with Matt, whose pace has become even more of a clumsy shuffle, now almost constantly veering off left. I was ready to insist on coming along, but Matt didn't even put up a fight to disinvite me.

Still, Matt wasn't very forthcoming with the docs, insisting he could tell the radiation was making him better and shrinking that tumor. It was a good thing Jenn and I were there to give more detailed answers to the docs' questions about his trouble swallowing, more frequent headaches, weight loss, extreme fatigue, worsening gait, and balance so lousy he sits down to pull on his pants.

I could tell Leibniz was concerned. Since he hadn't seen Matt at all since the start of radiotherapy, he probably could gauge the decline more clearly than any of us. He studied the original MRI on the big screen and said again, almost to himself, how he wished he could get in there and dig the damn thing out. Nilsson tried out a faint smile, acting as if this was another of Leibniz's crude exaggerations, and he assured us surgery remained impossible. "But we're hoping the radiation doses are keeping the tumor from the brain stem," he said, using a pencil to point out that rat's tail area of concern on the stem, where they hoped to halt the tumor's potential to block neural connections to the cerebrum.

Jenn asked if the surgeons had any input on a favorable date for their wedding plans in the fall.

"Let's look forward to end of this course of treatment after next week," Nilsson said. "We'll be better able to assess Matt's progress and set up the next stage of therapy. Unless the wedding involves a lot of advance planning, I would hold off."

"I hope you can be flexible," Leibniz said, exchanging a look with Nilsson and sounding so gentle, for him, that it freaked me. I yearned for him to be brash and confident like before.

Jenn, ever the improv champ, patted Matt's shoulders and smiled. "Oh, we can flex anything," she told them, "it's just going to be a little family affair in my folks' backyard."

"Perfect," Nilsson said. "Those are the best, no stress, no mess." He touched Matt's other shoulder, and we all laughed when we noticed Matt was having a quick snooze.

I walked with Jenn and Matt down to Radiation Oncology for his daily dose. Since I hadn't been to the Male Waiting Room for a while, I wondered how my lady friends were doing. Only two were there this morning, and I saw how they'd become friendly with Matt and Jenn over the past couple weeks.

"I'm sorry but Matt has stolen our hearts, little brother," the bold one said, "to the point where we're secretly plotting how to get rid of Jenn."

"It's a good thing you're keeping it a secret," Jenn said, smiling.

"How big she talks. But if I can beat cancer, I can beat any scrawny Junction chick."

I intervened to ask where the third of their merry trio had gone, the lady in the scarf. The quiet one looked away. The bold one stared at me, the jokiness drained from her voice. "Greener pastures, let's say. Last week, little brother, I'm sorry to tell you."

Back at home, while Jenn and Matt caught up via video chats with friends and family in Fruita and Grand Junction, I took advantage of the afternoon's cooling thunderclouds to pull weeds in Mom's veggie patch. Nasty invaders had crept into the kale, often disguising themselves in the shapes of the garden plants they invaded. The jungle growth of the tomato plants had hidden a whole new weed crop since my last effort.

I was running out of time to finish the house chores I'd planned to accomplish before the start of the school year. I wanted to impress Ted'n'Kathy when they got back in late September, but now I was staring down the first teachers' meetings in a week. Plus, I needed to start searching for a new place to rent, I hoped, by October 1. Meanwhile, the paint-blistered soffits over the patio stared down at me, looking crisper and more chipped with every passing hour.

"Need some help, little guy?"

Matt appeared under Ted's floppy garden hat, carrying the small white plastic stool he'd used in the shower five years ago when he fractured his right ankle in a biking accident. He set it in the far corner of the tomato patch, squatting to pull weeds sitting down. "I've been thinking how all my injuries, even just shin splints and pulled calf muscles, have all been on my right side, same as the tumor," he said. "Weird, huh?"

"Remember when Leibniz said you'd been fighting this tumor for a long time? It's been fighting you, too."

"Just my right side," he told me, adding that he'd been appalled by the long litany of symptoms Jenn and I had recited to the docs. He said he really hadn't been aware of what a fucked-up mess he'd become. "I think it's the radiation building up, knocking my system out of whack, and I didn't even fess up to the ones I was too embarrassed to mention, like how the little gasket in my dick has broken down, so I dribble a lot after I pee."

"That could just be old age," I told him. He laughed and attacked the weeds with great concentration, saying no way was he going to allow these alien aggressors to invade every inch of what Mom had planted and cultivated with so much love and faith.

❖

Aug 10

In the morning Matt said he felt better and even got up early, for him, to make scrambled eggs, fried potatoes, and toasted bagels. He didn't argue when Jenn wanted to drive him to his treatment again. Afterward, he skipped lunch and headed upstairs to sleep all afternoon. Jenn tried to lose herself in an apocalyptic Colorado novel, *Dog Stars*, which Matt had told her featured a mind-blowing scene at an abandoned airfield in Grand Junction.

So it was quiet, and I sequestered myself in the office, assembling my notes into a draft for Grumpy's deadline. Rough as it was, I finally felt I had a narrative that stretched from ancient geology to tribal and pioneer claims. From there, it followed the mine investors' first 70s intentions for Summitville all the way to the arsenic seeping unchecked and unclaimed down the Alamosa River in 1988. I needed a way to shape it all, or interrupt it with, ethical analyses of the crime using Strauss, Singer, and Sartre's viewpoints. For the first time, though, I felt confident I might get there, overcoming my faghood's inherent shallow limitations.

Toward evening, Matt appeared in the doorway, showered and dressed. He sat at Mom's desk just as I finished cutting and pasting my citations. With his wet hair combed, he looked a kid all ready for school picture day. Fingering one of Kathy's big bound botanical reference books, he sounded both nostalgic and philosophical, as if the long sleep had deepened his perspective.

He reflected on how proud he was of our

parents for their long careers in academia, their awards, publications, accolades from former students, and their original research, right down to the undiscovered wasp Dad had classified when he was still a grad student, *Euparagia devlinis.* Appreciative and assured, he reminded me of Dad himself, even parroting Dad's lame old pun about how it took an Irishman to help a WASP discover himself, and expressing more pride over how Dad switched from wasps to butterflies after Bush and Cheney invaded Iraq. Then he veered off into that wrong turn, that rough terrain of wondering if Mom and Dad were secretly ashamed of their oldest son for being nothing more than "a brain-damaged bike repairman and ski bum."

I told him it sure must be a well-kept secret, since all I ever heard was Ted'n'Kathy's worship of his good nature, sociability, agility, athleticism, prizes, and powers of attraction as a girl magnet. Imagine what a thrill it must have been for a high-school nebbish and a geek to have spawned an athletic champion and prom king. Matt then launched into a soliloquy about how proud they were of my teaching career and the importance of my Summitville thesis. I got embarrassed and told him to save it for my eulogy. He laughed, got up, kissed the top of my head, and told me it was sad, but he planned to be around to deliver it, then left me alone again.

❖

After he fought himself out of a sleep so deep he thought his head was being pressed into the pillows by "wicked ne'er do wells," Matt's expansive mood continued Friday morning. During breakfast, he praised Jenn's drama studies and her acting career.

"They're just commercials, Matt," she said, buttering everyone's toast. "I wouldn't call it a career. I even missed my chance to study Chekov and maybe land a part in *The Cherry Orchard.*"

"Man, I am so sorry about that."

"I didn't mean it that way. You got nothin' to be sorry about, Matt. I've loved being here with you and Luke in the old Devlin foursquare. When you're better and we're back in Fruita, I'll try out for something in the fall program."

"Maybe you've already moved beyond Mesa State," Luke said. "You might have to come here to the big city, get your Equity card, and work at the Denver Center."

Matt took the platter of scrambled eggs, but misplaced his grip and tipped it, sending a portion onto the table top. "Damn! Don't worry about it, I'll scoop up that serving. I'm not proud, just blurry."

Jenn seemed determined to steer the conversation away from double vision and other symptoms. "Oh God, guys, I have so much to learn, so much technique to study, not to mention my shallow grasp of the theatrical repertoire, all the great plays, classic and modern. I'm a dunce. A waitress. A scrawny chick from Junction."

"I think you're pretty va-va-va-voom," Luke said. "For a dang girl."

"I think you're just dang pretty," Matt said, leaning over his plate to kiss Jenn.

"And now you're Colorado's sweetheart, there in rotation every dang night on the TV."

"It's like Gail and Emily were saying, you've got that elusive something," Luke said. "You project a personality onscreen that's relatable and real. No BS."

"And yet, it's all in the service of BS. I didn't realize how fake it all was at first. It was even worse in Pittsburgh because I guess people there aren't as green, so the scripts were more aggressive, more misleading, about the actual environmental costs of gas and oil extraction. It's surreal, how producers thought I was just the perfect little Vanessa, the Colorado spokeswoman spreading her fake facts all around western Pennsylvania." Joyless, she laughed. "Thank God the money is good, huh?"

"Come on, Jenn. You're not doing anything but performing their lines. And hell yes, thank God the money's good. Otherwise, we'd be taking out a second mortgage to make my co-pays. That's why I've got to get back to Fruita this weekend. I can't let the shop go under just when we need the income most."

"They're going to shoot a new series of Colorado commercials soon," Jenn said. "I don't think you should worry, Matt. Plus, the staff can handle running the shop."

"But not the accounts and paperwork, baby."

"I think it's a good idea just to stay put this weekend, just till you're feeling better." She scanned the messy remnants of spilled eggs and shared a drooping smile with Luke. "One more week of radiation, then it's done and you can start stepping back into running the shop."

"I can travel four stinking hours. Come on. I'm not an invalid." He put his empty plate under the table's edge and brushed the stray egg pieces onto it. "This is just the accumulation of radiation. This is actually progress."

"Even though you've told me that twelve times since yesterday, baby," Jenn said, "I don't remember Dr. Nilsson ever putting it that way."

Luke made himself busy collecting the plates and cleaning

up at the sink. He was beginning to feel embarrassed, unwilling witness to their friendly but torturous disagreement. In the end, Matt insisted that he needed to "manage my life" in Fruita and Jenn lost the will to fight it. They took off for the Western Slope immediately after Matt's late morning treatment.

Luke started his day in the office by checking his email on Ted's computer. He didn't quite avoid reading the all-caps subject line of Jeff's latest message—I STILL LOVE YOU LUKE—before he deleted it unread.

❖

Aug 12

It killed me Marco was still so distant when I stopped by Emily's to pick them up for our Saturday morning bike ride. He'll speak to me, but only with the super-polite, super-reluctant syllables a kid that age feels forced out of him by inquiring strangers. Then he killed me again when he announced he wasn't going to join us after all, claiming he had a "conflict."

So Emily sympathized when we rolled off together down Twelfth Avenue to Cherry Creek and the Platte River trails. "Now you know how I feel," she told me. "All the little affections, all the desires to be close to me, to be included in my activities, that's all gone," she told me. All the middle school moms told her the same tale, how it suddenly changes at Marco's age.

Only two or three months ago, he would've been jumping out of his skin to come with us, I thought. Saturdays and evenings in the spring he and I were still playing catch on the diamond at East or sprinting on the track and excited in anticipation of another summer at the Congress pool. It made me wish again I could've somehow kept him from the big bad news of my homo-hood until he was older—and to have been smart enough to realize some of his macho cousins and uncles on the west side would be feeding his psyche with crude cracks about me.

All well-meaning progressives want to believe vociferous antigay attitudes are a thing of the past, that we wondrous urbanites are all post-homophobic, but I always knew that wasn't true. I've never heard gay coming-out advocates address the phenomenon of going through the trauma of coming out to family and friends only to have them forget their queerness, as if some self-willed denial wormed its way into their heterosexual consciousness. So, sometimes gay folks have to come out again and again to issue reminders and even assure their straight associates that yeah, they're *really* gay, that it isn't a phase or a voluntary change, like a bad dye job or a tattoo. I've had to remind colleagues and fellow grad students when they try to set me up with their sweet cousin Darlene that I'm really looking for sweet Daryl.

Do these little forgettings, these denials, arise from some unconscious disgust with the very possibility of gayness? As if it was easy to have to announce yourself in the first place, even to people who are distant acquaintances, as if straight folk ever had to do that, or be labeled a closet case. What about just being a private dude? I guess that's a luxury only shy straights get to enjoy.

Speaking of straight guys, what the hell is wrong

with them when it comes to appreciating Emily?
There she was, so freaking gorgeous in spandex,
her lovely rear propped up on her road bike as if to
advertise a happy future of sheer carnal luxury, all
of that sexual glamour wasted on me. Heads do turn
when she walks into a bar or a party, but turn away
as soon as they find out she's got an eleven-year-old.
She's so fit and speedy, too, a natural athlete like
Matt, and I struggled to keep up with her, especially
when we got to the last leg of our southward journey,
once the path passes the junkyards, light industry, and
sewer complex of Englewood and opens up south
of Littleton, that long stretch along the riverway to
Chatfield Dam where she torqued on the straight
stretches. I was huffing and puffing up the incline to
the top of the dam, too, a few hundred yards behind
her.

It was a clear, coolish morning with a blue
horizon over the Rockies, no threat of showers. The
season's been so wet that the wide open fields around
the oxbow ponds are still mostly green. When I was
a kid, bopping along with Ted'n'Kathy as we biked
down to Chatfield, I always thought this suburban
open space was true countryside, as if we'd ridden
so far from the city and into the green meadows and
little cottonwood copses, we'd reached Ireland or
some reasonable facsimile. Even now, I crave that
green landscape and, no matter how ludicrous it
sounds, mourn the passing summer even as it passes,
wishing I could somehow ingest the landscape or
at least smear it all over my willing skin like lime
sherbet before it all melts into school days and flying
snow.

I always get this way toward the end of summer, but it's more intense now because I'm burning away my twenties, too. I feel so acutely that deadline of my thirtieth birthday in a couple weeks. I keep thinking on the dread day I should be backpacking the Colorado Trail, another adventure I dared to fantasize with Jeff, or biking across the real Ireland, if only I had the money. Of course, I can't leave Denver anyway. Even after Matt's treatments end this coming Friday and he and Jenn head back to Fruita, the first faculty meetings start like clockwork that Monday. So, the summer that was so virginal in these pages two months ago is already tattered, worn down, and nearly done for.

I'm shocked it's Saturday night, and I still feel like staying home. (Damien: "So, tonight it's just you and the cat, like an old lady?") Am I really avoiding Jeff, who I thought I glimpsed Friday afternoon happy hour at Aunt Pete's?

Speaking of evil cats, Toonces has been pacing back and forth across the desks, sitting on the stacks of papers Kathy left clipped and tidy in trays before she left for Ecuador. He rifles through my own loose-leaf chaos of upheaved folders and reprinted articles, then wanders across my open, inert laptop, his paws dancing on the keyboard.

He's started this prowling nearly every time I sit down to write in the journal or search the internet or pound away at my Summitville draft. Either that or he obsessively circles the desk chair, stopping every now and then to paw the chair's arms as if he wants desperately to be petted or pulled on to my lap. But when I do, he fights me off and looks the other way as if I've offended him. It's like he craves attention, then shrinks from a caress. Only cats, of all creatures, seem to be aloof and needy at the same time. Though I wonder if that isn't a pretty good summary of my relationship with the world, especially my gay life.

❖

Sunday evening, Luke found himself in one of the old rockers on the front porch being psychoanalyzed by Emily and Damien, who'd stopped by separately and equally unannounced.

"Isn't this like high school?" Luke asked. "I love it, just hanging out, just random."

"This isn't random," Emily said from the porch swing she shared with Damien. "We've been planning this intervention all summer. So, Damien and I decided it was the perfect time."

"You've regressed to the nerd state that paralyzed you in high school," Damien said, still in his scrubbies, sipping a beer. Though he played now at being the intense counselor, Luke was glad to see him so relaxed after work. Usually, after a big Saturday night at the bars or cha-cha palace, then a shift of making rounds of terminal patients, whether transitioning to hospice or to the great unknown, Damien was either super hyper or super toasted. "This is why Dr. Emily and I decided to intervene. You haven't left your chambers for two Saturday nights in a row, Mr. Devlin. Terminal nerdhood."

"I should be so free," Emily said, "free to squander my freedom." Her mother had taken Marco and a crew of his friends to ride the roller coaster at Lakeside, his reward for washing Gail's car and watering her plants all summer.

"Quit yer whining, both of youse! I'm perfectly content in

my lonely singlehood." He raised his beer to them. "Except for the legal brews and the complete absence of parental authority, this summer has been like being stuck in some high school time warp, living at home, tethered to my big brother, tormented by my supposed friends."

"Here's my diagnosis, which I've been saving for my forthcoming *Dr. Emily Radio Hour*: your parents' optimism and sweetness launched you into a too-happy life, as beauty begets beauty. But you are also cursed to be something of an orchid child, fragile and difficult to bloom, prone to a terrible fall should you ever encounter the pain of the real world."

"Amen," Damien said. "Add to that your white boy entitlements. Heavens to Betsy, Luke, are you ever bound for a crash."

"Oh yeah! I do nothing but luxuriate in my privileges. We won't mention my struggles with Grumpy, my betrayal by Jeff, my rejection by Marco—" he said, cutting himself off, thinking of Matt, who was the only one of them who was really entitled to whine over his struggles and never did. "Or my exquisite lack of any known talents, intellectual, athletic, ecclesiastical, or retail. And now, my one asset, my shining youth, is about to be smothered in the ashes of my thirtieth birthday."

"Enough about that," Damien said tonelessly. "I myself wear thirty like a Technicolor dream coat."

"Yes, do get a grip," Emily said, who'd turned thirty in January.

"I just feel like I'm in a waiting room. I'm perfectly happy to stay, but I have to cross that threshold no matter what, and everything's unknown on the other side. I don't want to go, I like it here, I want to stay!"

"So, you're perfect?" Emily asked. "Luke Devlin, alone

of mankind, has achieved such perfection he cannot evolve more, learn anything else on the planet? He needs to retard himself, stay twenty-nine forever?"

"Like a big, clumsy, pathetic Peter Pan," Damien said, faux spitting faux disgust.

Luke didn't make a retort, clever or otherwise, because Emily's question caught him up short. He really hadn't thought of it that way, that the clichéd and universal clinging to one's twenties was really an argument for aborting development and experience. What else could it be?

As if to punctuate the question, the white *Book Cliffs Cyclery and Horsethief Adventures* van pulled up. Jenn double-parked and immediately circled the front end to open the door for Matt and help him climb down out of the seat. The three friends hurried off the porch and down to the curb with Luke crying out, "Matt, what's the matter?"

"Nothing…" Matt said, his eyes glazed and sleepy, his smile spare and quick. "Just lost my energy on the drive over the mountain."

Damien rushed in to take Matt's arm and help him up the curb. "Go ahead and find a parking space," he said to Jenn. "We'll get him inside."

As Emily reached to prop Matt up by his other arm, Matt let out a strangled laugh. "Did you dress for the occasion, Damien?"

"I wear these scrubbies day and night. Makes me feel like a big shot."

Matt bussed Damien then Emily each on the cheek and submitted to their help up the front steps. Luke walked down the block, following Jenn's short route to a parking space, then reached to help her with the overnight bags.

Instead, she reached for Luke, pulling him into a hug. Looking exhausted herself, she rested her head on his shoulder. "It wasn't just his energy he lost. He couldn't keep anything down all weekend. We even had to stop in Silverthorne and clean up a fresh round of barf."

"Poor Matt. Poor you!"

"I am such a selfish bitch."

"I've noticed that."

"No. Really. I resented him dragging us back and forth to Fruita for no good reason, even after I begged him to take it easy. He felt too weak to help at the shop or really do anything but rest at the condo. I don't have much patience left, Luke."

"Well, I'm glad Damien's here. Maybe he can advise us on anything we can do to get him in better shape for his treatment tomorrow."

"Doesn't he work in hospice? Oh, God, Luke!"

"He's a well-trained all-around medical guy," Luke hastened to say. They each grabbed a bag and headed toward the house. "It could be Matt has been right about what he repeated four million times last week, about the radiation building up and—"

"That's the other thing that's getting worse. Matt repeats himself all the time now, like he's not aware or paying attention to what he's just said."

"I guess you have a lot to ask Dr. Nilsson tomorrow."

"Come with me, will you, Luke, please? I'm afraid of what he's going to answer."

❖

Aug. 15

Yesterday morning was no damn good.

Jenn and I made coffee and breakfast as usual. When I went up to Matt's room to wake him, he muttered something about how he'd like to start walking to radiology again. I suggested we try that for when he was feeling better, but he repeated what he'd just told me as if he was talking in his sleep. There was slyness in his expression and for a minute I was relieved, thinking he was putting me on or performing some elaborate self-parody. I went back downstairs to help Jenn get breakfast on the table.

She was still castigating herself for agreeing to the pointless weekend trip to Fruita, and I told her I was still holding out hope Matt had reached some saturation point with the treatments and would start to improve.

So, when I heard Matt yelling for help on the stairs, I thought he really was joking—that he'd heard what I said to Jenn and decided to continue the parody performance in grand style. But he was in a heap at the bottom of the stairs, barefoot, still in his T-shirt and boxers, having tripped on the last few steps, or at least that's the most coherent explanation I could get from him. He landed hard on his right side, which would later bloom to a great purple bruise on his upper thigh.

Since he could barely limp around and needed our support to get up and get dressed, he finally stopped insisting we walk to treatments. Jenn and I helped him hobble to my car. I managed to snag a wheelchair for him at the hospital, surprised when he didn't refuse it. I was relieved because it was so easy to roll him into Radiology, but I was heartsick, too, never having imagined delivering Matt Devlin in a chair.

It got worse. For his routine nurse station

checkup in one of those little consult rooms, weight and vitals, the nurse did a double take on his weight loss and low blood pressure and had us all wait for Dr. Nilsson. Matt sank onto the examination bed. Under the windowless, blazing fluorescence Jenn fretted, picking up a *People* magazine, then setting it back down unread.

After a long wait, Nilsson and Leibniz joined us. Jenn and I both sat up a little straighter in those damn little plastic chairs, sensing hard news, while Matt dozed on the raised examination bed. Leibniz asked about Matt's decline over the weekend with a caring attentiveness that freaked me out. He drew Jenn into giving full details and gently pressed for even more, as if unraveling the thread of some neurological mystery. He didn't, as I expected, give any proclamations about probable pathologies, only confirming that the nausea, reduced immobility, and memory loss and verbal repetition were to be expected at this stage of brain stem pressure.

Nilsson, always more circumspect, was almost sheepish now. He gave a halting admission that the radiation treatments were reaching an counterproductive accumulation for the time being. The docs agreed they should stop and Matt should stay in the hospital for at least two nights for observation.

Leibniz flipped on a big flatscreen computer, and Nilsson killed the lights. It was A/V time in this cramped classroom, and our star student and subject was still in deep sleep, so Jenn and I studied the familiar MRI of Matt's brain stem tumor. Leibniz used a laser pen to circle where he'd hoped the dark mass would be reduced. Nilsson stepped up to explain that in many cases the radiation does halt the tumor's progress, but it had always been an open question with Matt's, considering the sheer mass, the remarkable aggression, the rapid growth. Leibniz reiterated that he'd love to get in there and scrape away, but while that would eviscerate the tumor, it would also end Matt's ability to function.

"End," Jenn repeated.

"I'm afraid so."

I didn't say anything to Jenn, who was clearly almost paralyzed with apprehension, but I had the strongest sense the radiation had been futile all the while. Not really a dog and pony show so much as a Hail Mary pass. The docs had held out hope and a proven methodology. It wasn't ever likely in Matt's particular advanced and delicate case, but they'd gone ahead out of sheer professional necessity. The course of radiation wasn't just fantasy football but the only alternative to the unbearable inaction of just watching my brother worsen and die. I'd wanted to believe in that final pass.

❖

Aug. 16

It's getting down to a few journal pages left. I hope I don't run out before the summer finishes me.

In the morning, I made an executive decision to contact Mom and Dad through their US sponsors in Tena and left an urgent message on the project's voice mail, which was just the beginning, I knew, of an elaborate process of messaging, calls, and canoe paddles to reach them in the wild.

Tuesday night, just as I finished writing the last entry, Jenn called to say she'd be staying with Matt at the hospital all night. She updated his condition since she and I had dinner in the cafeteria and I'd left them alone together: He was fully awake, wasn't on any sedatives, and was making more sense. His memory seemed better.

After the docs ran a series of tests in the morning, including another MRI, they decided there was no reason to keep him in the hospital, and Jenn brought Matt home after he was discharged around noon. The docs nixed any travel and wanted him back for a checkup after he rested all weekend. The discharge nurse issued him a cane to steady his balance on his right side and recommended no meds, just lots of rest and a "comfy bed on the first floor."

So, Jenn and I got the downstairs single bed ready, airing out the stuffy, cramped corner room, our official guest room since Damien lived with us after his stepfather kicked him out during high school. After he used his cane to get down the front hallway, Matt dozed on the bedspread while I set up the TV and a fan and brought down his shaving kit, tablet, and laptop. Toonces prowled every inch of the room as if claiming it for his expanding empire, then sidled up beside Matt's stomach, closed his eyes, and fell into the same drowsy rhythm.

I don't know why, but I was surprised when Jenn emptied Matt's upstairs room of all their clothes and toiletries, stuffed them in her duffel, and moved them into the guest room as if she were joining Matt on some stationary cruise. While he dozed, she busied herself hanging up his shirts and pants in the musty closet and setting up his toothbrush and razor in the downstairs bathroom. She didn't, though, unpack her own clothes from the duffel.

When I invited her to join me for a beer on the patio, she smiled, taking me up on the venue but not the beverage, finding a single-serve iced tea in the fridge. Jenn confided to me her concerns about the overpowering expenses of their high-deductible insurance. Though the radiation expenses would easily knock them over their limit, Jenn was devastated by the thousands and thousands she and Matt would have to produce just to meet the thousands more that would finally exhaust the deductibles.

She quickly changed the subject, as if embarrassed. Jenn told me her cousins planned to stop by tomorrow for lunch while they passed through Denver from their ranch on the Eastern Plains to attend to business and family matters in Grand Junction. She seemed tense about it. I didn't press her for details but said I'd make myself scarce if she wanted some family time with them. "Oh God no," she told me, "please hang out with us." She even bribed me with a promise she'd serve her famous pasta salad.

We both clung to Matt's test results and next checkup as if they were life rafts on this sudden cruise to the unknown. There was still a chance the effects of radiation therapy would continue shrinking the tumor. Ironically, now that he was done with the heavy dosages, he might generally improve. Maybe soon after he got lots of rest and the tests showed progress, they could pack up and head back to Fruita, where he could convalesce in his own place, maybe even put in a few hours a day at the shop. Right?

Matt felt good enough to get on his feet, shower, and act as Jenn's sous chef for a giant summery salad she assembled after I harvested masses of Mom's ever-advancing Russian kale. My phone sounded during dinner, at last, with a return call from deep in the labyrinth of stateside contacts with the Ecuador project. I took it upstairs in case Matt heard I acted unilaterally and against his wishes.

The project liaison told me they would do their best to contact Ted'n'Kathy, after making it clear it was only because I claimed it was a family emergency, and even then he sounded so reluctant to disturb the researchers' delicate, secret position in the Amazonian rain forest. Apparently, Mom and Dad had now joined another team working in an even more remote encampment than the earlier one on the Napo River. The request could reach them only via human messenger in canoe.

When I rejoined Jenn and Matt on the patio, they were in the midst of a joking fantasy about how they would install one of those sitting escalators for Matt so he could safely return to his upstairs bedroom. "Just put your cane on your lap, old dude, and let it whisk you away," Jenn told him, and it was so good to hear them both laughing.

Staring up, Matt then wondered out loud if it really was as hazy as it seemed to his blurry vision, and we noticed an orange overcast had glazed over the night sky. After dinner, we put on the early local news channel and discovered massive wildfires were out of control in both New Mexico and Idaho. Though Colorado was still saturated from monsoonal storms and fire-free, Denver was the epicenter of smoke from both those distant blazes. Everything was blurry to everyone, a reddening fog smothering the stars.

❖

As Jenn's cousins settled around the patio table just past noon, Damien stopped by to check on Matt just before he was due to disappear into a twelve-hour shift. "I'm starting to think you wear scrubbies all the time," Luke told him.

"Join the club." Damien shook hands with the cousins and excused himself, saying he was hoping to see a much-improved version of Matt today. "Then I gotta hustle straight to hospice-land."

"Damien happened to be here when Matt collapsed," Jenn explained after Damien went inside. "We were so lucky to have him here because we were majorly freaked out."

Her cousin Dan, a big, fortyish blond guy in a red cap, lowered his voice. "Is Matt going to be okay alone with him poking around in the bedroom?" He laughed, pointing inside. "Isn't that little black guy just kinda, you know, fa-la-la?"

"I think Matt can handle it," Jenn said, her jaw clenched. "Damien's been a family friend since, like, forever."

Dan's wife, Tracy, slapped her husband's arm. "Honest, he's such a redneck. I don't know if he's fit to bring off the ranch and into the city."

Dan smiled through his immense tobacco-stained choppers. "I admit it, I'm uncouth sometimes. But damn, Jenn, are we ever proud of you for these commercials. You're like a movie star out in Lincoln County."

"Lucky me." Jenn auditioned the smallest of smiles. "Who doesn't want to be the belle of Punkin Center?"

Tracy laughed. "Last I checked, Punkin Center had a complete shortage of any belles whatsoever."

"We're all hoping we can sell mineral rights to frackers, believe me," Dan said. "I wouldn't mind being a millionaire. Meanwhile, your TV spots are sticking it to the greenies but good. Coming across so honest, but sweet as pie. Everybody in the county loves you, cuz."

"What I want to know," Tracy said, tapping her lips with a napkin, "I mean, besides your recipe for this excellent pasta salad, is if Matt's going to be all better in time for your wedding in September."

"Well, we never really set a firm date."

"But you know the family grapevine, Jenn. On social media they've practically got you hitched already, there's so much excitement. Everybody loves a wedding, right? And I know your mom is over the moon that you're going to have the ceremony in Junction."

Luke realized he'd almost forgotten about the wedding plans. They'd become irrelevant, like worrying about the tide schedule during a tsunami. He decided to wade in and rescue Jenn. "Matt's had a few serious setbacks with his treatments. We're just crossing our fingers we see some progress soon."

"We might have to wait until later in the fall," Jenn said. "I'll post something if that helps keep the family at bay. We've got to keep our eyes on Matt's recovery, and I'm under contract to film a whole new series of commercials, so…" She shrugged. "Hey, would you guys like another beer?"

Dan nodded, but Tracy stood up, shaking her head. "We've got to drive over the mountain, sweetheart."

Dan swigged back the last of his beer. "How come you're not drinking nothing but that foofie iced tea, Jenn? You getting too refined for us rednecks?"

"I am, Dan, but that's not the reason," Jenn said, standing to take his arm, easily joshing him now. "You know I love beer, but I've got to watch my figure these days. I'm on a diet for the camera. It's merciless, you know."

"Nobody ever looked better in front of that merciless camera," Tracy said, embracing Jenn and wishing the best for Matt as she hustled Dan from his ain't-that-the-truth-cuz? squeeze and, with fond farewells, said goodbye.

"Whew," Jenn said, easing back down among the remnants of pasta salad, fruit and cheese, and empty bottles. "I wouldn't mind something stronger than iced tea right now."

"I mix a mean gin and tonic," Luke said. "You deserve it."

"Thanks, but I really do have to watch the alcohol. Nothing's more fattening, right?" She patted her stomach. "I'm starting to get a little paunchy down there."

"You're as slim as a tiger."

"Anyway, Luke, now you've had a nice taste of my family."

"I liked 'em."

"Dan's brother moved to Leadville right after high school. He had to commute over Tennessee Pass for construction jobs down in Vail after the moly mine closed for the second time. You know those huge slag piles left behind right in the center of town? He and his wife let their kids play in 'em even after the EPA declared them a toxic site, just to show 'em. That's my kin."

"It's tough on the mine workers and the roughnecks in the energy fields when the jobs disappear. I get it."

"They don't. They don't adapt, Luke. They just bitch and attack the environmentalists. If the EPA tries to clean things up, they're the bad guys, the guv'mit, not the corporations that are ripping them off. Anyway, I'm kind of embarrassed for my family. You'll see for yourself when our wedding finally comes to pass."

"Matt and I are Colorado natives, too, you know, with a buncha cousins in the countryside. We're not all foofie fa-la-la as this little broken branch of the city Devlins you're hitchin' yerself to."

Jenn laughed, swigging back her iced tea with a Dan-like swagger and forcing a belch. Then she wiped her mouth demurely and kissed Luke on the cheek.

❖

August 18

It's been a restless day. Matt insisted on joining us for breakfast, acting all proud that he shaved, showered, and shuffled onto the patio, dragging his right foot and steadying himself with the cane. He hardly touched the pancakes Jenn put in front of him, nor much of my special gourmet contribution, scrambled eggs. But he sat there smiling his new leftward drooping smile at our small talk—Mr. Normal, Mr. Charming—munching just enough to make it seem like he had an appetite.

When Jenn jogged to City Park a few hours later, Matt retreated into his downstairs room and asked me to help him go through his emails and social media accounts. I scrolled through all the messages and read them aloud, which was a great afternoon diversion except that I discovered two major deceptions of Matt's: He couldn't read anymore because his blurring and double vision made it too hard to focus, and he hadn't really informed his friends or our out-of-town cousins about his ordeal. He had a backlog of puzzled messages from his employees in Fruita, each pressing him for more detailed information about his diagnosis and treatment and when to expect him back, the same from a coterie of new friends in Grand Valley, and even more from his old friends in Denver. Matt was overwhelmed by how to respond to them all and worried people would think he was shutting them out.

"You *are* shutting them out," I said, recalling so many instances lately when he was chatting with some of these folks by phone, audio only, his voice strong, his humor good, and his wit intact, but his words evasive and answers incomplete. I wondered who they must envision on the other end of the line, nothing like the drastic reality of the blinded, skeletal, half-paralyzed stubborn being performing on his smartphone.

His withholding and secretive approach was another form of closet. Like the gay closet, it demanded energy from everyone in on the secret and ended up forcing them into a closet as well.

I suggested we compose a mass update by email and social media posts. He nodded and told me he'd think about it. He could really use my help writing it and getting it out there, and I could tell his eyes were glazing over with fatigue. His words were getting a little slurry and incoherent. Before he fell into dozing, he said he didn't want to be overwhelmed by visitors, and he didn't want to get too tired or have people get too concerned about how lousy he looked. "Maybe wait till I get better," he muttered. "We could have this big reception in the backyard, beer and music and everything before we move back to Fruita." Yeah, maybe even celebrate their engagement. Finally give people a date for the wedding. Yeah.

With Matt drifting off, I shut off his laptop. Jenn had been standing in the doorway, still in her running clothes, swiping at her eyes. "I'm dribbling sweat," she said. "Sorry if I stink. Funny how strangers kept staring at me, mostly tourists up at the natural history museum. Then they'd get excited. It's good old Vanessa, the Fracking Girl! Look, she even jogs, just like a normal person. They'd stop me, jamming their faces beside mine for selfies."

As if we were on some kind of family relay, I clasped her hand in mine, changed into my running clothes, and ran three and half laps around Cheesman Park. Near as I could tell, no strangers stared, requested selfies, or got the least bit excited to see me panting down the path.

After a cooldown when I got back, Emily and Marco had angled kitchen chairs into Matt's room while he and Jenn sat up in bed. I stood in the doorway, listening to them reminisce about the raft trip we'd all taken on the Arkansas through Browns Canyon last summer, the first time, in fact, I'd spent much time with Jenn.

Matt gently teased Emily about how she'd freaked out over a major rapid and fell inward when she should've been high-siding. Marco asserted he wasn't afraid at all and kept his eyes open through the whole hysterical lunge into whitewater, which he thought was a total blast. Matt told him he was proud of the way he kept digging his paddle through the rapids, just like he should. When Matt looked at me, Marco noticed me there, too, and made that sour *aw shit* face he'd been using to greet me all summer.

Matt caught that look, too, and a shadow seemed to cross his brow. "Hey, Marco," he said. "I suggest you stop with this bullshit, kid."

For the rest of the visit Marco studied the battered old slats of the wood floor but never looked at me.

❖

Kathy Devlin's staticky voice sounded on Luke's phone early Saturday. He was groggy and she was wide awake, even hyper. "Luke, did you really say it was a family emergency?"

"Mom, it really is." With his crazy piled-up wavy bedhead and puffy eyes, Luke was glad they weren't on video chat. "It's serious, and I want you to prepare yourself for some very bad news, okay?"

"Oh God, Luke, are you and Matt all right? My head's been swirling since two contact people in Tena, then our native allies tried to get word to us on this godforsaken river island. It was crazy, hooking up to the satellite phone out here."

"It's Matt, Mom." He realized how long they had left them almost completely in the dark, just jollied along with vague reassurances. "It's a true emergency, and it's going to change everything."

"Okay, okay," she said, turning away for a moment. "Ted? Ted! Luke has something serious to tell us."

❖

Late Sunday morning after Jenn helped Matt with the toilet and shower, then showered herself, she called Luke into the guest room. Brushing her own and Matt's wet heads, she patted the bedspread to invite him to sit beside her. "I'm sorry to leave you alone with Matt for the next couple days, but I don't have any choice. Our savings are about zero, our checkbook is in minus territory, and I've got to get over to Fruita for a few days." She had to meet with the film producers about the shooting schedule and help balance the books at the bike shop. "I might even wait tables at the steakhouse for a night or two if I can get a gig."

Luke looked at the duffel she brought from Matt's room, never unpacked. "Hit me up if I can help with the mortgage or hospital bills or whatever."

"If I do have to ask for a loan, it'll be just until the money starts rolling in from the production company again."

"Don't worry about it. I'm loaded after living here at Ted'n'Kathy's all summer."

Jenn clasped his hand. "I know. High school history teachers, you're all such moneybags." She turned to Matt, smoothing the hair she'd just brushed. He lay atop the covers, sitting up on the pillows but slumped to his left side. "Thanks a million, Luke, but I think things are going to work out. They're gonna get better, right, Matt?"

"Wish I could go…with you, baby," Matt answered, caressing her arm. "Wish I could help out."

"You can, baby. Just take care of yourself and keep fighting. We'll get there, I swear."

They kissed, slow and sad, and Luke left them alone. He nuked some leftover coffee and took it to the front porch. It was almost as stuffy outside as in the guest room. Smoky skies still settled over the city from the Idaho fire in the inaccessible Frank Church Wilderness eight hundred miles northwest. He

thought of Ted'n'Kathy's memories of how bad Denver's smog
was when they were kids. Every point of light, the windows
opposite, the windshields, even the silvery undersides of the
maple leaves bounced back orange and fiery, and the air itself
felt claustrophobic.

"Just a sip for the road? If you don't mind my cooties."

Luke passed the cup to Jenn, who'd appeared beside him
with her duffel and a bulging daypack. "I can get you a travel
cup."

"Naw, thanks, I'll stop for a latte in Dillon or Vail. It'll
break up the drive. Don't forget all those frozen breakfast
burritos and the huge vat of pasta primavera left over in the
fridge. You shouldn't starve."

"You're gonna make one helluva sister-in-law."

"I'm just sorry I have to leave you all alone here. With
Matt, I mean."

"I'll be fine. Meanwhile, you take care of things in Fruita
and don't worry about us."

"Yeah, I better get going." Jenn hugged him sideways,
refused his help with the duffel, and hurried down the stairs
then out to the van. "Be back soon as I can."

Luke leaned against a porch post, watching the van as Jenn
turned westward onto Thirteenth Avenue and disappeared.

Inside, the house felt airless and dark. It hadn't seemed so
alone and desolate since those first rotten days after he'd kissed
off Jeff Douglas. As horrible as the reason was, having these
weeks with Matt and Jenn had been full of camaraderie and
that larky spontaneity that comes with brother and sisterhood.
Sleeping in their own rooms, swilling coffee over their favorite
breakfasts, then walking a few blocks north together every
weekday—it was like being kids again, only with a bit of adult
appreciation for each other, not to mention thicker skins—but
these walks had an ominous terminus.

He checked on Matt, conked out on the swayback guest room double bed, snuggling Toonces. Matt snored, still in the clothes he'd put on after his shower as if he had somewhere else to go.

Luke sat on one of the ancient chrome kitchen chairs left in place after Emily and Marco's visit and listened to his brother's struggling breaths, hearing something new, a kind of catch to each inhale. Come on, what the hell was the reason for that? Matt's lungs were probably pink and perfect, great athletic bellows that powered him up and down fourteeners and single-track inclines that had mere mortals pushing their mountain bikes. What were Nilsson's exact words, *total system failure*?

"Knock, knock? Anybody home?" It was Gail. She ducked her head into the room, then eased in, bearing a newspaper and a garden bouquet wrapped in a cone of Sunday ad copy. "Daisies and rudbeckia, nothing compared to your mother's, but who's competing with some smart-aleck botanist?"

"That's what I always say." Luke lowered his voice to Gail's hospital-room sotto voce and patted the seat next to him. "I gave up competing with Mr. and Ms. Perfect years ago. I decided it was better to be just what I yam, their special needs child."

"Me too, their *special* friend. Handicapped by terminal ordinariness." Gail sat, eyeing Matt. "He looks so young, Lukie, with that big, wild cloud of brown waves and eyes closed tight, those adorable eyelashes. He looks just like a puppy in a box."

"At least Jenn got him washed, soap and water and everything, I presume."

"I can hear everything you're whispering," Matt said, eyes still closed, stage-whispering. "And I agree, you both are special. Very special."

"Well, I'm going to try to read you the stories in the news section," Gail said, opening the paper edition of the Sunday *Post*. "I'll sound out some of the tricky vowels and consonants with your help, Matt, then move on to the sports pages—scores only, for easier reading—and your favorite, the funny pages."

"Read me everything but *Family Circus*," Matt said. "I hate that crypto-religious cutesy crap."

"Oh, that's my favorite!" Gail cried. "Especially when the dead grandparents reappear as pseudo-angel-ghosts. Luke, please put my flowers in a vase, then get your hide out of here. It's the last day for the Congress pool, you know. Grab your trunks and get over there. And take your time, I'm just going to read *Family Circus* over and over until Matt conks out again." She laughed, then turned to Luke and winked, unfolding the funny pages.

❖

August 20

I loved Gail for spelling me this morning while Emily and Marco attended Mass on the west side. The truth is, while Jenn stayed here, I haven't really put in much time as Matt's primary caregiver, but that's probably going to change till she gets back.

So, it was closing day at the outdoor pools. Summer unofficially ends for me with the last whistle from the last lifeguard on the last minute of the outdoor pool season. It officially ends when teacher orientation meetings start at seven thirty sharp Monday.

I couldn't stop myself from dedicating my last mile in the lap pool to Matt. I said this little incantation to the gods of nature: *Please transfer my health and strength back to him.* More irrationality surfaced when I dried off and sunbathed for a short while on the pool deck and had an almost hallucinatory sensation. With many Sunday dads and moms present and the kids contained and calmer in family units instead of the mass chaos of weekday daycare mobs, there was almost palpable harmony. I heard laughter, not yelling, the kiddies trying to paddle into parents' waiting arms, not so much splashing warfare. The fiery lighting and the slight blurring the smoky air caused made everyone look somehow exalted. I sat there, almost paralyzed with appreciation behind my sunglasses, wondering if this was how it was in the afterlife, in heaven, everything serene and playful, even haloed in the haze, the love and attachments so obvious and easygoing.

But of course it was anything but eternal. As I left, I almost tiptoed out, afraid to break the spell, trying not to envision the Congress Park pool emptied in a few days, a barren concrete basin, trying not to foresee the deck and kiddie pool drifted with snow and ice in a few months.

❖

After a long, quiet Monday assembling his draft notes into paragraphs and the Summitville crime timeline into ethical frameworks, Luke alternated between the desktop computer upstairs and his laptop on the kitchen chairs beside Matt's bed. Matt claimed he wanted to hear sections of the draft, so Luke read them aloud, and Matt offered a question or suggestion, sometimes dozing off in mid-paragraph.

For lunch, Luke readied some of Jenn's pasta, asking Matt if he wanted to have it at the kitchen table or patio. Despite Luke's offer of an arm to help guide him out, Matt stared at his cane wistfully and took a long time to announce his decision. "I think, just today, I'll rest some more, okay? Can I have it on a tray here in bed?"

"Coming right up, Mr. Devlin," Luke told him, trying out a jokey smile and bringing a bowlful to the bedside for himself, though he wasn't really hungry, freaked out by Matt's difficulties swallowing. Finally, it was easier to scoop a few small helpings into Matt's mouth with a spoon.

But Luke had to excuse himself, making a production of cleaning up the bowls and silverware at the sink, hoping the running water drowned out the desperate, helpless sound of his sobs.

Midafternoon Luke put aside his draft, which was rough but semi-complete, and prowled Matt's upstairs room for books, finding their old favorite in a well-worn boxed set, the *Lord of the Rings* trilogy and its slender companion volume of *The Hobbit*. It had been a Christmas gift from so long ago that the tag stuck to the box still said "To Matt and Lukie from Santa."

So, in the heat and muggy wildfire smaze of August, the room fan whirring the pages, he read aloud Bilbo Baggins's adventures one more time, that ancient prequel they'd loved to tatters on long snowy weekends. Luke was glad to see Matt sat up straighter for most of it before sinking into his pillows and falling back to sleep when Bilbo reached the endless confusion and dullness of Mirkwood.

Early evening, Emily stopped by still in her work clothes, all Ms. Insurance Agent in a light blazer over white blouse and a light, summery skirt. Along with a moveable feast of eggplant parmesan Gail had stashed in the fridge, Emily had the day's *Post* on her tablet with the Monday Sports Extra and a willingness to continue reading Bilbo out of Mirkwood as necessary. "Yes, I do take after my mother after all, Devlin boys, so withhold the sarcastic commentary. Be gone with you, Luke, go get some fresh air and exercise."

Luke hopped at the chance to get into his running shorts and dash across Cheesman, then toward the downtown YMCA. Their family membership at the Y was going to waste while Ted'n'Kathy were in Ecuador. He'd stop in for a quick upper-body workout before jogging home. It wouldn't take that long, he reasoned, but would make him feel like his shoulders, pecs, and abs wouldn't completely atrophy.

Taking Logan Street north and crossing Colfax, Luke ended up on the steps of the Basilica of the Immaculate Conception. Five thirty Mass was already over. With no advance plan or explanation he himself understood, he tried to enter the cathedral as a sweaty pilgrim in skimpy shorts and a tank top. To his surprise, the massive doors were locked.

He pulled each handle in disbelief. He had an unshakable, untested, childish faith that Catholic churches never shut their doors. What were you supposed to do if you needed to pray, or more urgently, confess, at some oddball time—like seven at night on any given Monday? As a kid he'd been dragged to the Basilica for the big holy days or whenever his mother was feeling spiritually grandiose. Even though Good Shepherd was their parish in ordinary time, and he hadn't been to Mass in quite a while and only then to keep his mother company, Luke felt a proprietary kinship with the cathedral. And now, in his hour of need, it had locked him out?

His hour of need. What was he doing here? What kind of hypocrite was he, anyway, a long fallen Catholic with no claim on the faith? What force was pulling him to pray for Matt, to light a pay-to-pray candle and hasten the long darkening of the

Enlightenment with more hocus-pocus and magical thinking? The same one, he was sure, that led him to dedicate his last summer laps at Congress pool yesterday to his brother's health. It was lousy, being an agnostic existentialist hypocrite. What he wouldn't give to pray without irony or self-castigation, to believe without second thoughts his prayers could stir God to mercy.

It was growing dark, the final third of August slashing the long summer evenings shorter. The businesses on the cathedral's shabby neighboring corners were already lit up while taillights trailed a crimson procession down Colfax to the Capitol. Luke sat on the highest step as more of the corner's ever-present homeless folk gathered around him. Some said it was always busy with the homeless because they felt welcome and safe on God's very front porch; others said they were attracted by the charitable services; still others that it was a convenient spot to panhandle for the fast food and liquor shops nearby. What the hell, he didn't have a clear reason why he was sitting here, either, cooling down in his running clothes, resting his elbows on his knees and dropping his head to his open palms.

An older, heavy woman rifled through a trio of canvas shopping bags. She stopped to stare at Luke, then continued rifling. A youngish, full-bearded guy adjusted the trash bags piled in his shopping cart and tied smaller ones on the rim like panniers. Where would they go after dark? Even on a summer night, it would be sleeping rough, curled up in a doorway or concealed on a skanky mattress behind some alley dumpster. Luke could not imagine the desolation of not having a room of one's own, let alone a cheery family house that was, and apparently always would be, waiting to enfold him no matter how many leases he lost—a room of his own always available for one night or a week or a season or a lifetime.

He glanced to the opposite corner, Logan and Colfax, where he had waited at the red light so many times while silently cursing the motley shufflers in the crosswalk who made him miss the yellow light or halted his right of way on the green.

"They sometimes lock the front doors after evening Mass," the older lady told him. "I think they're afraid of drunks sleeping it off in the pews. Are you all right, son?"

Luke tried a smile that must have looked horrible and forced because just as he formed it, he realized he was crying. He thought with shame of the secret contempt he'd ever held for anyone, whether for lack of smarts, for extreme body types, for the transgression of being very old or homeless or severely disabled. His breathing and heartbeat had steadied now. Swiping off the tears, he relived that strange vivid yet unreal clarity that overtook his mind just as it had at the pool Sunday, only now it was the homeless, not the kids, who seemed to breathe with him in harmony, as if all the troubles and discomforts they faced could be subsumed in a moment like this, as if each one tasted the same hope in the heedless, inequitable heart of the city.

He imagined this common force breezing in on the oncoming dark all around him, breathing into the assisted care midrise behind the Basilica where Kathy had taken her boys on holiday visits to shut-in family acquaintances and distant relatives, floor after floor of little apartments sheltering the elderly and disabled. The imaginary breeze crossed the city center to the indigent encampments on the South Platte River, the makeshift plastic walls or piles of old sleeping bags hidden in the coyote willow, where scattered shirt sleeves billowed like waving arms, a benediction for everyone.

Luke rose and headed up Logan to Sixteenth Avenue, where he decided to skip the Y and just jog back home. Emily had been Matt-sitting long enough, and though he might not have worked out any upper body muscles, he had exercised his mind's most untrained corners.

❖

The next evening, catching a cross breeze from an early evening thunderstorm, Luke opened the journal at the kitchen table. He could see into the guest room, where the fan still swirled medium fast in the window and Toonces snoozed atop Matt's rump. Matt was sleeping, too, as was Damien, upright in one of the kitchen chairs, *The Hobbit* tossed aside on the other. Luke hadn't had the heart to wake either of them when he got home from the university just now.

❖

Aug. 22

This afternoon, Damien did me the great favor of staying with Matt for a few hours after his long shift, the last one before his vacation started. I had an appointment at the History Department, where Grumpy had arranged to transfer the care and feeding of my thesis back to Dr. Buster Levine, who'd returned from his leave. It should have been joyous relief for both Grumpy and me, but like my last encounter with Grumpy, it was surreal, this almost out-of-body experience of being under the authority of someone whose dislike of me was so implacable.

Buster hadn't yet arrived, and while Grumpy waited in the conference room, I avoided him in the History office during a late afternoon rush of staff and professors crossing paths. It was the end of summer session with only a few weeks before fall classes started. Renata rose from her desk as soon as she saw me and pulled me into a hug and kissed my cheek. The department gossip mill had spread the news about Matt somehow, because I hadn't told anyone directly except maybe sideways in emails to other grad students.

"I've been praying for you and your family," Renata told me, offering what help she could to ease the pressure of my deadline and department paperwork. The modern US history mafia, Drs. Tod Ramirez, Dottie Killen, and Tyrone Pinckney, stopped shuffling through their summer mail to offer similar kind words. Tod, who's barely a few years older than I, pulled me close and actually roughed my hair. As he did, I spotted Grumpy leaning outward in his chair, straining to see what he'd been listening to in the office. The kindness of Renata and my past professors clearly bedeviled him; he scrunched his forehead and practically harrumphed.

Dr. Buster Levine arrived with his usual flurry of loose papers flying from the fold of his laptop, his mop of blond-brown hair askew, his neat button-down untucked over old cargo shorts flecked with paint, and a thousand apologies for being late.

He shook hands with Grumpy and pulled me into a brief, manly hug without explanation, indicating for me to sit beside Grumpy. He praised Grumpy for his assistance during his absence. Buster opened my draft on his laptop and thanked Grumpy for—he was sure—helping to make it such a unique and pertinent history thesis. Certainly one of the most fascinating and Colorado-specific bodies of research and ethical rigor he had yet seen.

I sat stupefied as Buster scrolled through my draft, highlighting my analysis of the Summitville crisis as filtered through the ethics of Strauss and Singer, but especially commending the sections of Sartre. I breathed relief, almost smelling the incredulity in Grumpy's sweaty discomfiture.

Buster said he went ape over how I tied in not only the geologic history of the mine's region and the Euro-human history going back to the 1590s but also my overview of mining practices in Rio Grande County, then dug into Sartre's concept of bad faith as the mining company allowed eighty-five thousand gallons of contaminants into the watershed. And the title, *Bankrupt at Bitter Creek*! Buster pushed his laptop aside and turned to Grumpy. "Raymond," he said, "I think you have shepherded not just first-rate research, but an unusual, publishable master's thesis."

I almost laughed out loud at the idea of my being a lamb in Grumpy's loving summer pasture. I kept my head down, though, jotting down their ideas for the revision. When I rose to go and lingered at Renata's desk to say goodbye, I could hear Grumpy say to Buster, "What doesn't add up for me, Levine, is all this fawning over Mr. Devlin. I was made to understand he lacks

Luke put down his pen across the journal's last page. He would have to write the summer's last entries starting backward on the final pages' reverse sides. The video chat box suddenly opened up on his tablet. His mother wasn't smiling or laughing, and even in the small low-res image, Luke could see the tense cords in her neck. "We're in Panama City, waiting for a connection to L.A. Then an all-nighter in the L.A. airport. We'll catch a six a.m. flight to Denver. How's Matt? How are you, Lukie?"

"I'm doing fine. Matt's about twenty feet away in the guest room. See?" He stood and took the tablet closer to the doorway to catch a shot of Matt, Toonces, and Damien, all still fast asleep.

"I would love to talk to him, but we should let him sleep if he needs it."

"Yeah, he needs it. He's become like Toonces, Mom, sleeping most of the day away. He's still recovering from that massive dose of radiation."

"Is he doing better, then?" His father crowded into the chat box. "Hi, Luke!"

"Hey, Dad! I wouldn't say better, but he's getting plenty of rest, and Damien, Emily, and Gail are all helping out. Lots of casseroles and even a surprise pizza from the cousins. Matt liked that."

"Is he eating well?" Ted asked.

"Well, he's hardly eating. Like, he had barely one slice of the pizza. He has to be careful when he swallows."

"It doesn't sound so—"

"Hang on, Dad." Luke had to cut off his father because Damien was calling him, his voice straining, high and loud.

❖

August 23

I'm writing in the hallway outside Matt's ICU at two in the morning. There's an alcove near the huge floor-to-ceiling plate window open to the fiery darkness with sofas, coffee tables, and lamps, a serene, well-appointed little anteroom for the noisy purgatory of intensive care. From six stories up, the skyline downtown is blazing weirdly close and indifferent, and I imagine all the night crews in those high-rises, preparing the offices for transactions officious officers will achieve no matter who lives or dies.

When Matt collapsed on the guest room floor, the commotion woke up Damien, who thought Matt might have been trying to reach the kitchen to join in on the phone call. I had to sign off to help Damien with Matt and couldn't make contact again. Mom and Dad had already boarded their flight to L.A. I hated leaving them mid-emergency, adding to the inner turbulence of the last leg of their long journey.

Nor could I reach Jenn, leaving messages on her phone and with her parents, who weren't sure why she wasn't at the condo in Fruita unless she had picked up a shift at the restaurant. But the restaurant said they hadn't heard from her, either.

Damien and I decided to call an ambulance since Matt was completely incapable of walking or being walked to my car. It was almost as if his legs were paralyzed. During the brief wait for the EMTs, Damien alarmed me even more with his CPR-like movements to get Matt to breathe regularly. The first thing the EMT's did when they arrived was to give Matt oxygen. All through the rapid rescue scene, watching the medics hustle my brother out of the house on a collapsible gurney, his muzzle in a respirator, my addled brain kept repeating Nilsson's warning: *total system failure.*

In the ICU before midnight, after hours of touch and go, Matt finally stabilized, his consciousness wavering, his vital signs weakening then leveling as he struggled to breathe normally again. He had blood pressure cuffs on each arm, billowing like a bellows as they sent data to the multiple screens and bleeping numbers that surrounded him. He didn't talk, but whenever he startled awake, the alarmed expression in his eyes implored me to tell him what the hell was going on.

Dr. Nilsson checked in periodically, and I held on to any threads of hope in his assessments. Was this a common reaction to high radiation doses? Dr. Nilsson shook his head, saying that this was more common to brain stem pressure, the tumor literally choking off his brain from his nervous system's functions. Matt's legs and lungs were like stranded soldiers marooned from their commanders, awaiting orders no one could send or receive.

❖

When his parents landed in Denver at eight in the morning, Luke updated them on why he dropped the earlier call and all that had happened since. His father tried to insist they would take the A train, and Luke could pick them up downtown at Union Station.

"You guys are not taking the train, Dad, not with your luggage. This is no time to be green. I'm picking you up at the airport. I'm already on my way." Ted relented and passed the information on to Kathy.

Luke could hear her cry out. He waited, and then he asked

his father to pass the phone to his mother. "Mom, are you all right?"

"I'm glad Damien and Emily are there. It just shocked me, Lukie, that it's so dire."

"Yeah. I'm sorry now I went along with Matt. We disagreed, but I chose to honor his insistence we keep all of this from you. He wanted to wait and give you good news about his recovery, but now it's even worse than before he collapsed, when I talked to you from the house. Mom, you and Dad have got to prepare yourselves." Luke stopped, wondering if he should wait to tell them in person, on the long drive from the airport. He decided no, enough with the mercy of omission. He had to be direct and give them a chance to absorb it before he got there. "Matt's not just reacting to the radiation now. It looks like the treatment couldn't halt the tumor's advance. Now it's closing in on his brain stem. We could lose him."

❖

With the wildfire smoke clearing from rain and steady breezes, Luke could spot glaciated snow patches on the Arapahoe Peaks on their way into the city from DIA. He stopped himself from mentioning it to his parents, who rode in his car stunned and silenced. Normally Luke looked forward to spending an hour comparing climbing notes with his father, each one blatantly exaggerating summit exploits, but now he wouldn't dare. With each of them shell-shocked by the full impact of Matt's mortal condition, Luke could never let Ted'n'Kathy know that he'd almost been killed by lightning and his own stupidity on that summit.

Leading his parents to Luke's room in the ICU, Luke wished he could spare them the visual drama of the emergency wards they passed through, the hustling medical staff and the groaning bodies on gurneys, the faces of waiting members of other families, their faces paralyzed in disbelief and tormented concern.

Amidst it all at the end of the hall, Emily appeared in the doorway, tall and dressed for work at the office. She smiled grimly, her mouth about to crumple. Kathy, small and compact and absurdly tanned, dissolved into Emily's outstretched arms.

"I had this huge welcome-home party planned for the fall," Emily said, letting her tears fall. "I never imagined your homecoming in this goddamn hallway." She pulled Ted into the embrace. "Let's go in. They said family members only, so I lied and told them I was your daughter."

"How is that a lie?" Kathy asked, hesitating at the doorway. "You're actually my favorite daughter."

"And mine," Ted said, who stood back now, too, balking, as small, slender, and bronzed as his wife. On each side of Emily, they looked more like her sun-struck children.

Inside, Damien was in his scrubbies, helping the ICU nurse adjust Matt's blood pressure cuffs. Matt's head leaned off the pillow, which was about to fall, so Damien gently shuffled it back and readjusted the feeding tube taped to his arm. Damien sidled closer to Ted and Kathy, pecking their cheeks. "He seems to have slipped further into unconsciousness this morning," he said. "He hasn't spoken or responded to us for hours or ingested anything."

The nurse smiled her greeting. "That's why we're hydrating him, that's why he's hooked up. It's just a saline feed."

"Can he hear us?" Kathy asked, easing herself closer to Matt's side.

"We don't know," the nurse said. "Go ahead, Mrs. Devlin, you can sit on the bed."

Kathy did, smoothing her son's hair. "He looks so thin. So young." Touching Matt's face, she said, "I love you, Matt."

Matt stirred, shaking his head and raising his chin without opening his eyes. Ragged, loud, he cried, "I love you, too, Mom!"

The five crowded around the bed seemed to breathe together, then catch their breath, waiting for more. But Matt never opened his eyes and seemed to sink into an even deeper, stiffer sleep.

Luke wondered if those would be his brother's last words.

❖

August 24

Mom and Dad are sleeping in their own bed for the first time in months. Completely exhausted by the flights and the trauma of arrival, they went to bed right after our early dinner, lasagna courtesy of Gail, before it was barely dark. They're calling this a nap and planning to head to the hospital later tonight. They really don't want to leave Matt's side.

We haunted the ICU waiting room all day, Mom telling everyone Gail was her sister and Marco her nephew. The staff must have been suspicious of the ever-expanding diverse group—including Damien, who went home to change into street clothes and returned as my stepbrother.

Poor Dr. Nilsson. When he met with our self-declared family in the late afternoon in a crowded consulting room, I don't think he expected a public speaking engagement. He avoided the word "coma" when he discussed Matt's condition but suggested no further treatment. He stressed how unusual such benign brain stem tumors were, especially for Matt's gender and youth, and specifically of such large size and aggressive growth. He wanted us to know that he and Dr. Leibniz had considered every known course of action, and only the daily doses of radiation had held any possibility of forestalling total breakdown of functionality.

When my dad asked how that would manifest, Nilsson seemed even more compact and pale, a wispy, wistful version of his already frail self. He said the likely scenario would be a shutting down of Matt's lungs and cardiovascular system.

"So, he'll have a heart attack?" my dad asked.

"More like a heart stoppage," Nilsson said. "Even if that doesn't happen, he might completely slip into a coma-like state without assistance from IV feedings." Nilsson wouldn't say it, but I got it: comatose. Matt would simply dehydrate and starve to death.

Nilsson told us he understood from his medical administrator that Matt already had an advance directive with a no-resuscitation clause. Emily, Gail, Marco, and Damien exited without comment at this point, the make-believe family showing more intuitive grace than most blood relatives. Depending on how long Matt survived without feeding, he could be placed under hospice care and have visitors from outside the family, Nilsson told us, wan and sad-smiling.

I felt so bad for him, I embraced him. He held on to me, so tiny in my arms he made Dad seem like a lumberjack.

That was that. Mom and Dad and I went back into Matt's room together. They planned to head home for dinner and nap before coming back later. I watched them watch Matt for a while and decided to leave them alone with their beloved boy. I made the excuse I had to powder my nose, but gave away my ruse when on impulse I bent down to kiss Matt on the forehead. That elicited a moan from my mom, followed by a loud cry from her heart, pure and terrifying, such as I have never known but am sure I will hear forever.

It wasn't my nose I had to powder but inner turmoil I had to silence. My psyche seized with unstoppable tremors of anxiety, I bypassed the quartet in the waiting room and continued across the hospital's vast reception hall, past the concierge station and the café fronting its pretty garden courtyard all the way to the chapel.

I sat in the back pew, under the gaze of the plaster savior and attending saints. I fingered a pamphlet I found among the missals, *When a Loved One Is Gone...* Only one other person was there, an older Latina on her knees, praying aloud in sweet, solitary Spanish. She rose, taken aback when she noticed me, and then she smiled. I smiled back. When I heard her footsteps retreat on the hallway's tile floor, I began to bawl big, sloppy tears. The whole process weighted me so bad I had to lay my head on my hands as I steadied them on the pew's railing in front of me. I stayed like that, shaking with childlike sobs, for a long time. I couldn't get the echo of Mom's cry out of my head.

When I was done sobbing, I was ready to confront

Christ. I stared straight into the stony eyes of the statue, molded to look all benevolent and forgiving. Fuck that, I told Him, I don't forgive you, you son of a bitch!

Then, when I was done cursing the son of God, I pulled down the kneeler and fell to my knees. Pressing my hands together, as I had done as a Catholic schoolboy, I prayed hard, telling Jesus I really didn't mean it and begging God to spare my brother's life.

I heard footsteps in the chapel's hollow, harrowing silence, knowing she would find me this way, but I didn't care. Emily entered the pew without a word and knelt beside me, kissing my cheek and swiping my cheeks and nose with a tissue. Then she lowered her head and offered prayers of her own that God, I'm sure, was much more disposed to hear.

❖

Luke played hooky from the second day of teacher orientation and made Ted's favorite breakfast, corn fritters—really Matt and Luke's time-honored kiddie recipe of pancake mix with canned corn gooped inside. His parents came home before sunrise and fell into another short sleep. They were anxious to get back to Matt's bedside, but in the meanwhile, flipping the fritters and setting the table for his folks, Luke took an odd joy in their company, dread and trauma mixed with the simple pleasure of reunion. Dazed, sipping their coffee and clearly starving for the fritters, Ted'n'Kathy looked sun-kissed and long-haired, aging flower children fresh from a long vacation. Luke was sure their tans hid what would otherwise be a splotchy, pale distress.

As his folks devoured the fritters, Luke brought them

up to date on his master's work over the summer and gave a dramatic narrative of the struggle with Grumpy and the triumph with Buster. They, in turn, related their tale of good and evil in the Ecuadorian Amazon, how their species identification team was like a rescue mission on the run, their locations frequently changing to foil oil company informants. It all had an exciting but daunting theme of collecting data that at best would build the case to save disconnected remnants of wildlands from extinction and exploitation, or at worse would catalogue the wipeout of unique life forms in Eden.

"It was so strange under the circumstances to plunge back into the States as if we landed in the hospital itself," Kathy said. "I'd gotten used to the clinic in Tena—one of the few modern health facilities in the entirety of the Oriente region— and yesterday in the ICU with Matt, I felt like a native woman bewildered in the bustle and technology. I took little walks to stretch my feet and explored so many corners of the emergency ward, distressed by the sheer discomfort of so many patients and so many resigned or terrified families. Like ours. Not normal human illness, but such extreme internal damage, all so far from any hope of real health or wellness. Even if technology was lacking, the Tena clinic was more alive with healthier people at all stages of life. Often here there's no suggestion whatever of what constitutes health itself, or a good life in that sense, and certainly not good dying."

"Jesus, Kathy. Would you rather Matt were in that clinic in Tena," Ted asked, "or here in the big bad American hospital?"

She touched Ted's hand, then grasped and kissed it. "The big bad hospital, for sure. But still I felt so overwhelmed and detached from the processes of salvation, you know?"

"I don't think salvation was ever promised, darling."

Luke listened, thinking of how overwhelmed and detached he felt in the chapel, and he wondered if faith was even supposed to bring us back to attachment, and what salvation meant in the context of modern medicine.

"Well, however alienating the processes are, I felt buoyed up by our family and our family of friends," Kathy said. "Our tribe. That was lovely, Luke, having Emily and Damien with us. And Gail and Marco. But I sure missed having Jenn there."

"We saw her image on ad kiosks at the airport, looking so gorgeous."

"And sincere."

"Then I caught three or four of her commercials on the TV in the waiting room."

Luke nodded and waited for their comments, or at least their questions, about what the hell she was doing as the nation's sweetheart, this Vanessa who was shilling for the Council on Clean Energy. But Kathy just sighed. "I just wish Jenn would get in touch."

There hadn't been any phone messages yet, and neither her parents nor anyone at the shop knew where she'd gone. Luke decided there was no point leaving more voice mails if she didn't pick up. Without much hope, he checked for texts on his phone, still finding none, then scrolled through his inbox, though he hardly ever exchanged emails with Jenn. "Wait, here's something!" He deleted another all caps I LOVE YOU subject line message from Jeff Douglas unread, then read Jenn's email aloud: "'I'm so sorry I've been out of reach. I did receive your messages, though, and I'm on my way to Denver.' She sent it fifteen minutes ago."

❖

After another round of meetings at the high school, Luke returned home for late lunch with his parents, each of them stunned to silence by the next slap of bad news at the hospital.

Matt had officially slipped into a coma. He was taken off IV feeds, respirator, and all monitoring connections, but he would remain under observation. If, after a few days, his condition remained stable, he would be transferred to home hospice care.

Damien had already set the patio table in the deep shade of the oak. "The cheese and avocado sandwiches I made with my own bare hands, people. But the potato salad is your favorite, Kathy, pure supermarket deli."

"No, kid, I insist on gourmet—" Kathy tried to joke, but couldn't sustain the performance and ended up in Damien's arms, holding back sobs and resting her head on his shoulder.

"It'll be okay," Damien said, patting her back. "I wanna be Matt's hospice nurse. Okay if I move back into the guest room for a while?"

Kathy steadied herself, leaning back, her hands on Damien's shoulders. They were exactly the same height— twinned, Luke thought, in shrimpiness. "It's still your room, Damien. I've always saved the posters of Foxy Brown and Don Cheadle you had up in there, safe for your return."

"Come on," Ted said. "We appreciate this beyond words, but it's your damn vacation."

"This is a perfect damn vacation. It'll keep me off the streets, right? And remember, I'm your stepchild now."

"You've never stopped being our stepchild. Who else but immediate family would know my secret shame about supermarket potato salad?"

"If I'm your stepson now," Damien said, "do I have to go to Mass with you?"

"Hell yes," Kathy said. She smiled, but Luke could see how she forced down a few bites of the sandwich and salad before setting her fork aside. Ted munched half the sandwich and moved the salad around on his plate, declaring it was good. Then he excused himself and, without explanation, rose and walked into the side yard.

After a short while, Luke did the same, following his father around the house on the flagstone walk squeezed between their wall and the fence next door. He found him leaning on the exterior wall, hands on the bricks, head upturned, inspecting the soffits. "See there, son?" He pointed up, casual as anything, as if he'd been expecting Luke's co-inspection. "Those blisters where the gutters meet the edges. I'm sure the flashing is causing leaks. Maybe it's loosened somehow under the shingles. It's just chipping paint now, but we've got to get it fixed before the damage spreads."

Luke moved closer to his father, looking up. "Yeah, I do see."

"I just don't want...I don't want the damage to go untended, Luke." Ted looked down, still steadying himself against the wall, letting his eyes rake the ground for paint chips. Then he shoved off and seized Luke in a side hug.

Luke pulled him to his chest as his father began to shed tears, his face pressed against Luke's shoulder. "Stupid soffits," Luke said, patting his father's back. "Stupid damage."

❖

August 25

I'm alone in Matt's hospital room past midnight. He's breathing steadily, if a little rugged, but he hasn't awakened since that moment when he blurted those words to Mom. Jenn stayed at his side for hours this evening, though he didn't stir. I hope Mom and Dad and Jenn are getting lots of sleep at the house.

I'm officially writing on the back pages now. I guess I'll get as far as I need to this way. I don't know why, but it seems like all this should be in one volume. And I sure don't want to start a whole new journal until somehow life gets normal, whatever that is, let alone better.

Midafternoon, Jenn drove up to the house in her little compact. Her parents were following in their pickup. My folks went back to the hospital with Damien, leaving me and Jenn to be the welcoming committee, which made me nervous as hell.

Jenn's dad is a heavy man, inert, wary, watchful, and wordless. Jenn's mom is a serious religious conservative who doesn't approve of me at all. Not just because I'm a homo but because of my big mouth. When I first met them at a BBQ in Junction, she started in on a rant about how the United States of America was the most generous country on earth, giving away all of our hard-earned taxes on foreign aid to countries that weren't even Christian. I was sitting beside her, enjoying my single slice of American cheese and bright yellow mustard on a white flour bun, and just had to comment, in my winning dumbshit way, that in reality the USA had one of the lowest rates of foreign aid of any rich country, a fraction of one percent, and that a lot of that tiny fraction did in fact go to Christian countries in Latin America and the former Eastern bloc. She wanted to know if I was calling her preacher a liar and why I hated America. That was basically the whole of my acquaintance with the good lady so far. I knew later she asked Jenn if it was right an avowed homosexual should be teaching teenagers, and wasn't there some way I could be saved. She suggested getting-straight Christian therapy programs if it wasn't too late for someone of my advanced age and so deep into my sin.

Jenn gave me that let's-just-be-calm-and-endure-this look when she led her parents inside, and then she busied herself catching up with Toonces, who fawned on her, if cats can fawn. I'd prepared a snack with carbonated sugar water drinks, but her old man preferred a beer, and I was glad to oblige and join him. Jenn's mother thanked me for the snacks and remarked over and over she was sorry Jenn had vanished like that. She didn't know about us, but she practically had a heart attack wondering where on earth her precious daughter had disappeared to. When they reconnected with Jenn and found out more about Matt's condition, they just had to come support our family and would keep praying for a miracle.

As a recent involuntary prayer-for-miracles myself, I couldn't argue with that. I extended my hand and thanked her for coming; she clasped it and teared up. Jenn's dad broke his silence. Revealing a bald pate with gray hair clustered at the temples, he took off his cap and held it close to his chest.

"I lost my brother when I was only thirteen," he said. "Leukemia. Never got over it. My prayers might not mean as much, since I'm not really a churchgoing man, but I'll try." I thought amen, brother, and offered to get them settled in Matt's room. I suggested Jenn take mine and I'd stay at the hospital, but her folks were staying at a relative's, so I offered to drive them to the hospital where they could see Matt and spend time with my parents.

I shot Jenn my own let's-just-stay-calm-and endure-this look. My parents have been worried, too, I said, because they love Jenn so much. But who doesn't? Jenn's mom looked at me quizzically, then smiled. She said she never noticed how much I looked like Matt, and how much I sounded like him just then.

❖

Straight from school meetings, Luke joined Damien, Jenn, Kathy, and Ted the next afternoon. The plan was to transfer Matt to home hospice in Damien's care in the early evening; there was paperwork, there was a consult with Dr. Nilsson, and there were offers of end-of-life and family grief counseling for a few hours before the transfer. Luke brought his jogging clothes in his school pack. He was crazy for an hour of fresh air and exercise before facing Matt's transfer.

While he changed in Matt's room, he glanced at that copy of *The Hobbit* they'd started on Matt's last days at home. Damien must have brought it along on one of his own all-nighters. The open page was facedown on the nightstand. Bilbo and his allies are confronting goblins and wargs, the last of the complacent little hobbit's confrontations with demonic forces and circumstances of a reality far more complex than he'd ever imagined. Luke fingered the open page, never dreaming he'd never get another chance to finish the damn book with Matt. He touched Matt's arm and told him, "I'm jogging around City Park. I'll be right back."

Even though it was sunny now, thunderclouds had cooled the air enough to enjoy the play of light and shadow along the Sixteenth Avenue bike lane, the light oddly filtered. Despite the clearing blue skies, Luke wondered if there was more distant smoke on the horizon from new wildfires he'd lost track of. He followed Sixteenth until it dead-ended smack into the steps of the high school. He half loved and half deplored the signs of school's first days, stray teachers lingering at the entry or going to their cars with laptops and armfuls of notebooks, football teams in practice formations on the fields.

It was quiet in the park, though, except when he reached Ferril Lake and could see where crowds roamed in front of the planetarium at the Museum of Nature and Science. He ran up the hillock and joined several family and daycare groups, where swarms of kids seemed to be staring into smartphones, laughing, all at once. No, they weren't phones; they were cardboard viewing devices handed out by the museum. One young dad said we were having a partial solar eclipse. "It's happening right now! Look at the shadows."

He followed two boys and their mother toward the deep shadows of a stand of trees just south of the planetarium. The brothers were too young to care about being cool, holding hands as they skipped ahead. When they reached the shadows, they laughed, dancing around as the canopies shook in the breeze. "Look, mister! Little moons!"

Luke looked more closely and realized, sure enough, the entire shadow was not a solid mass but a connected mobile array of crescent moons. He laughed with the boys and copied them as they caught the crescents in raised palms open to the shadows. As Luke eased back to the crowd, he saw that every shadow, whether of a person or a shrub or a wall, was composed completely of tiny crescents. Then in a further sweep of the sun, the crescents closed into solidifying shadow. In unison, the mob of kids lowered their cardboard viewers, letting out a collective sigh.

"So, the moon's just passed over the sun," a planetarium volunteer announced. "Did you all get to watch the moon's impression disappear?"

As the crowd drifted away, Luke stood on the museum's concrete perch, his favorite view of the city. The high-rises downtown emerged just beyond the lake, behind the dock-like bandstand and pavilion, and the late afternoon light brightened, hazing out the jagged line of the Great Divide to frame the city skyline.

He ran straight down the hill, knowing he had to cross part of that expanse, those leafy old blocks east of downtown that had always nested him, snug between City Park and Capitol Hill where he'd lived his entire life. It was like passing through the tunnels of his own bloodstream, warm and familiar and inevitable. "It's my home," he murmured without meaning to, "this is my home." He shivered, oddly lonesome, a brief chill jolting him, like an icy shiver stabbing the heat. His breath caught as he ran exposed in the blazing post-eclipse sun.

He decided not to circle the park but to return to the hospital via Twenty-First Avenue. He sprinted then slowed, steadying his hard breaths as he eased to a walk for his cooldown, again with anxiety not blood seeming to pulse through his veins.

Emily intercepted him in the hallway before he could reach Matt's room. "He's gone," she said, even and quiet. "His breathing stopped minutes ago, Luke. He's gone."

❖

Saturday morning, the house felt emptied, but Ted'n'Kathy were asleep upstairs and Jenn hadn't yet stirred. Luke took his coffee into the guest room. He sat on the bed he'd made up for Damien. He'd welcomed him by hanging up those old movie posters of Foxy Brown and Don Cheadle Kathy had saved, a harebrained gesture he'd hoped would earn a small smile.

But Damien wouldn't need the room now. The hospital bed he'd ordered for the front parlor had been canceled. Matt's body had been whisked from the hospital on the same kind of gurney it had arrived on, off to be cremated.

Toonces hopped on the bed, prowling the spread, then the pillows, then back to the spread. When Luke reached to pet him, he dodged his hand and let out a high-pitched cry, then kept circling the bed until he stopped dead center.

❖

After Emily, Marco, and Kathy returned from eleven o'clock Mass on Sunday, a small klatch of first cousins stopped by the house with birthday cards and a couple pizzas for lunch, Luke's favorite Veggie Gourmet, each with a small candle in the center.

Luke was surprised, but he wasn't up for it. He hid his unsociability by playing bartender, opening wine. and rooting around in the fridge for beers and the big vat of Bloody Marys Judith dropped by earlier. Jenn stepped in as hostess, inviting everyone to gather on the patio and putting out paper plates and napkins. But after grabbing drinks, the cousins insisted Luke sit center stage at the patio table, blow out the candles, and enjoy the first slice. He opened the silly cards, most of them variations on turning thirty as a horrific tragedy, and he kissed the girl cousins and shook hands with the boy cousins. There was so much sadness under their laughter and joshing that Luke felt torn between appreciating their effort and wishing they'd all leave him alone. This was what love was, wasn't it?

Once Emily, Marco, and Jenn started playing dodge-car

Frisbees on Vine Street, the cousins joined in, though being Sunday there were few cars to dodge. Marco exhausted himself trying to out-defend a neighbor kid, and Luke felt like sitting out the second round of show-offy maneuvers, with Emily executing Olympic-quality moves in her church clothes. He found himself watching from the front steps beside Marco. "Your cousins are a lot more fun than my dad's cousins," he told Luke without prompting. "We hardly ever have pizza," he said, "and nobody plays Frisbee."

Luke turned to look at Marco, marveling at his normal tone and ordinary words, which he hadn't heard in almost three months. "Anybody play soccer?"

"Just the guys who grew up in Mexico. They'll play soccer anywhere, anytime." Marco laughed. "Like the supermarket aisles. Or, like, the weedy lot beside my grandparents'. The weeds are so tall they can't find the ball sometimes."

"Sounds more fun than Frisbee."

"Yeah, but most of them aren't like that. They're always playing games on their phones or watching TV."

"Look at your mom. You and her could inspire those slugs to get off their butts!"

"Naw. We've tried. I think they're afraid of my mom. Like, being shown up."

"It does hurt a man's pride, a dang girl being so good."

"I remember this time when I was little and Mom and Matt blew everybody away. We went to the soccer field at Lincoln High, and they just kept scoring all the points. The Mexicans couldn't believe how good they were, for gringos. They called Mom *la Reina Rubia* and Matt *el Rayo Muerte.*"

"The Blond Queen and the Death Ray?"

"Yeah." Marco fell silent for a while, watching the Frisbee players. "After that, Matt, he got so involved with Jenn. So then I started thinking about how you and Mom were friends since you were little kids and liked each other so much."

Luke watched Emily jump to catch the disc and artfully spin it on. "You thought she and I might get married? Is that why you got so mad at me?"

Marco just nodded.

"I get it, Marco. I'm gonna stay best friends with your mom, but I won't ever be your stepfather. But I will be like your big brother, if you let me. I always will be." Rising, he held out his hand for a manly shake. Marco took it and ran down the stairs to rejoin the Frisbee players.

Inside, Luke meant to score a beer and pass through the kitchen, where an older cousin with a blond comb-over and an angry tone appeared to have entrapped Kathy and Ted. "So are you gonna press malpractice charges against this Nilsson quack? And that big-shot Jew? Promising Matt that BS about a cure, then probably killing him? Lukie, you know what I mean, right?"

"No, Donnie, I don't know what you mean." Luke got a beer and shut the refrigerator with a deliberate slap. He stood in front of Ted'n'Kathy as if to guard them from Don. "I think without the radiation we'd have had two months of even faster decline. Plus despair without any hope. I think it was the only option. It was one that Matt freely chose. Dr. Nilsson never misled us or made promises. Would you like a beer?"

Donald passed on the offer and clammed up. Luke went out to the yard, emptied now that the cousins were playing Frisbee, and took a moment by himself on the bench in his mother's Old Lady garden. Among the now-spent lovage, bitten-up hollyhocks, and flowerless phlox stalks, he could hide from the grief-stricken birthday merriment and sulk. There was this strain in his family that reminded him of what Jenn said of her cousins in Leadville, the ones who'd urged their kids to play in toxic slag piles just to show the Environmental Protection Agency.

Show it fucking what? How little they thought of public sector scientists? Or how little they thought, period. They'd reflexively mock and blame wildlife experts for dwindling species and health advocates for banning their favorite carcinogenic additives. The nation's history, too, would be just fine if historians would stop seeking the truth about it. Without a trace of shame, these angry voices would blame meteorologists for hailstorms.

One of his two favorite scientists approached on the garden path. "Geez, Luke, you look so pissed off," his mother said. "You're not letting Donald get to you, I hope?"

"He's being such a horse's ass."

"He's always been a horse's ass, so what's new?" She sat on the bench beside him. "The garden looks wonderful, by the way. Thanks for taking such good care of it."

"All I did was water and weed. It was your creation."

"I had a little help from a whole array of greenhouses and garden shops. And grandmothers. So," she said, folding her hands in her lap, "Father dedicated Mass to Luke. Emily arranged it."

"Sweet. What did I do to deserve it?"

"Okay, to Matt."

"Even sweeter. You always did that, you know, mix up Matt for Luke and Luke for Matt when you were calling for us to stop doing something, then you'd throw in 'Jack-Pete-Mike!' to cover it up. LUKE-MATT-JACK-PETE-MIKE!"

"It was always good for a cheap laugh."

"Mom, I gotta tell you something. I thought about it all night. I know it's survivor's guilt, but it's still valid. So, I'm not saying this to guilt you or elicit sympathy, just to get the truth out, okay? I think you and Dad have gone through hell learning about Matt's tumor so late and having to come home in such a panic, then watch him die, Jesus! But you've also been cheated even worse than that. I just don't think I'm... like, adequate to take the place of Matt." He choked on a breath, getting it all out in a rush. "I mean, maybe the wrong son died."

"Oh!" Kathy cried out. She put her arm around Luke and put her head on his shoulder. "My poor baby."

"No, really, Mom. I'm not asking for sympathy. I can't stand to watch you guys suffer. I didn't think it was gonna be like this somehow. I just imagined *my* grief, *my* loss, you know? I just didn't foresee I'd be grieving for your grief, too. I just don't know if I have enough space in my cardiovascular system to contain it."

"It's the same for me, Luke. I'm trying to keep from drowning in my own rivulet of pain, then I see you and Dad and Jenn awash in the same vortex beside me, and I just... Well." She patted Luke's unruly mass of hair. "Just please don't say that, don't think that way. You'll kill me, too. There is no such concept as the *wrong son*."

"But you know, there is, because I idolized Matt just the way you and Dad did. So did everybody else who ever got to know him. He was my favorite person in the world. There was no role for me to fill but second banana, but I never minded. It's not guilt or a non-concept, Mom, it's just the way it was. And now you're stuck with just me, the klutzy one, not just the second banana, but a *gay* second banana! What a freakin' drag for you and Dad. For starters, there's never gonna be grandkids."

"I don't know where to start, Luke, except that I thought you were the smart one, but I must have been wrong. Let me set you straight. So to speak."

Luke laughed without wanting to. Kathy clasped her arm in his. "There was never such a concept, not a hint or an unspoken whisper of all that, even in the most private conversations between Ted and me. In fact we always had a private joke, calling you Matt'n'Luke, all one word, because we thought of you as one unbreakable unit. We always loved the way you adored Matt and the way Matt took you in his arms. We looked at other brothers, always at each other's throats or yelling at each other, or just other people's messed-up kids, and exchanged our sighs of relief and gratitude for our wondrous Matt'n'Luke. So don't you dare ever wonder about that, Luke, not ever.

"And being gay? Come on, it's part of you. You wouldn't be you if you weren't gay, and I love *you*, so how could I not love that you're gay? Love is not an endangered species. So buck up. You're thirty now, and you should know however life is going to evolve, there is no quota, no shortage, no threat of not enough love to go around. I never had to choose which of you I loved more, only to feel this limitless fondness. Matt—I mean Luke—Jack-Mike-Pete—love is infinite, Luke. It's infinite."

❖

By evening. the fridge groaned under a near infinity of casseroles. All afternoon neighbors and friends and relatives had stopped by with covered dishes, and now, Ted'n'Kathy joked about the Festival of Carbohydrates: lasagna, mac and cheese, scalloped potatoes, baked ziti, eggplant parmesan, and pasta primavera. At the table, partaking freely of proffered wine and a smorgasbord of noodles, Jenn and Luke and Ted and Kathy joshed that if they could hold the memorial tomorrow, they wouldn't need to order any more food. "Too bad tomorrow's Monday," Luke said. They had agreed on a Saturday memorial at the parish family center.

"And what about his friends in Junction?" Jenn said. "A lot of them are stuck at work on weekends. Not to mention my family."

"Why don't we have something over there, too?" Luke said. "Maybe at your mom's church?"

"God no! Come on, let's not bring crazy into it. Let's just pick a Sunday in September and have a picnic at Reed Park in Fruita."

"I've been thinking, too," Luke said. "We could canoe out and spread some of his ashes at Horsethief Canyon."

"Amen! He loved that section of river, so much."

Luke thought of his first exposure to the Colorado River canyons when he'd visited Matt and Jenn's condo in Fruita, just in June. He remembered how she'd mentioned earlier men in her life, roving ski bums who'd left her behind: *I didn't sign up for that.* So she'd thrown in her lot with the one ski bum who settled down and loved her but still left her behind. "Are you ever gonna tell us where you disappeared to?"

"I was just holed up at the condo, not answering any phone or texts for a few days. I did stop by the shop, where they've all kind of adapted to Matt's absence but just need a bookkeeper. Then I had to deal with the producers. They want to move up the shooting schedule for the next Colorado batch of commercials. But mostly I was just hiding, from you and your family, from my family, and most of all from myself. I was just inert, after Matt went comatose, inert and panicked at the same time, very weird. A better person would have stayed at his bedside, but I freaked out." She pushed her bowl away. "I'm so sorry."

Kathy reached to cover her hand with hers. "You don't owe anyone an apology."

"I just believe I didn't measure up. I wanted to be alone, licking my wounds. Luke, I remember you were telling me about your thesis and, was it Sartre? That concept of bad faith—how does that go again?"

Luke was reluctant to answer because he felt bad for Jenn and her spiral into self-castigation. "It's…inaction and evasion instead of commitment to the best course of action."

"Right," Jenn said. "I think that's the real evil, that wallowing around in self-pity and being paralyzed."

"You've been trying to survive under immense pressure," Ted said.

"Just remember," Kathy said. "You couldn't have brought more happiness to Matt."

"Jenn, you need to appreciate how much you helped *Matt* go forward," Ted said. "After he met you, he finally stopped screwing around and going from girl to girl and resort to resort. He was committed to you and the business. And your new life in Fruita."

"We've taken so much comfort," Kathy said, "from your presence in Matt's life."

"Not to mention relief," Ted said.

"I think you've handled this whole damn catastrophe with a lot of grace and generosity," Luke said. "I'm glad you were here with me, Jenn. You can't blame yourself."

"And you can grieve any way you want," Kathy said. "You can put polka dot panties on your head and prowl the streets of Denver screaming."

"You'll fit right in on Colfax," Ted said.

"Or hide out in your condo for a month or a year. Or a decade," Kathy said. "It's your grief. But we'd love for you to stay with us for a while, if you'd like to. Make Matt's room your own. Maybe even transfer to a theatre program at Metro

State this fall. I'm just being selfish, Jenn. I always wanted a daughter, but God sent me snails and puppy dog tails."

"You're always so wonderful," Jenn said, "as usual, you guys. It's lovely, but I'm not a Devlin. I'm not lovely. I really am Grand Junkyard trash. First of all, okay. I'm pregnant, and since Matt was declining so fast I spent a lot of my disappearance thinking about aborting. Explain that one, Luke, when action not inaction becomes bad faith?"

Kathy reached to take Jenn's hand again and held on tight.

Jenn stared straight ahead, at nothing or at something unseen. "I had an abortion when I was sixteen, okay? My deep dark secret. I never even told Matt."

"Wait, go back. You're not trash, Jenn, and I'm speechless," Kathy said. "A baby!"

"Which I am going to raise and love, but my God, what have I got to offer? A mortgage I can barely pay unless I figure out how to manage the shop and keep making commercials."

"We love you no matter what," Ted said. "You've got to let us help."

❖

Everything went fine early Monday morning. It was an abbreviated schedule for freshmen and new students, letting them find their classrooms and meet their teachers. Luke only had two sections of freshmen, so he had some time to prepare his classroom and materials for the week ahead.

Emily appeared at his classroom door at lunchtime, bearing a surprise—sesame tofu from his favorite Thai place. She wore a visitor's badge over her office costume, which was fussier and flouncier than usual. Beside his desk, Luke vogued for her his own uniform of button-down and khakis. "Look at us, Em," he said, "honest-to-God thirty-year-olds, all grown up."

They carried their takeout boxes to the same spot they'd lunched in as students, in the shade of huge fruit trees on the Esplanade. "It's always hard to believe summer is over," Emily said. "Tomorrow, this whole place is going to be overrun with students thinking the same thing. Did you stick with your journal every summer day?"

"Pretty much. Sometimes I summarized a few days together, but I kept with the plan to note the passing of every one. I can account for every summer day."

"Any conclusions?"

"If you keep a journal to capture time's passage, it'll just show how fast it all goes by anyway. It might also show how hapless we are, how helpless we can be in really shaping our fates, how unpredictable and horrible life can get. At least now I have an inkling of what you went through when you lost Carlos."

Emily fell silent for a long moment. "Your summer could not have started more carefree and ended more snarled in heartbreak." She touched Luke's shoulder. "I'm sorry I brought it up. Meanwhile, prepare yourself," she said, getting up and straightening her skirt. "You're going to have a surprise visitor this afternoon."

❖

After lunch, Luke chatted with a few last stray transfer students, and then he was completely alone. Feeling a little glitchy and directionless, he decided to check on some map files.

Standing there, rifling through a drawer, the dead weight of the week ahead overcame him. The hundred and fifty students he would encounter on Tuesday, then again on Wednesday. The five different classes in three subjects he needed to plan for, to have a coherent hour of instruction ready for each one. For the first time in five years of teaching, he stood frozen in astonishment, unable to believe how much he was called to do, the complexity of a single day's activities, the impossibility of meeting thirty students at a time, five times a day every day, each with a name and a backstory and a personal mode of learning or resistance to learning. How had he ever done it for a freaking day, let alone a week let alone a year? How the hell was he ever going to face tomorrow?

He couldn't comprehend the future now that Matt was dead. How was he supposed to proceed through life without his brother? How he was going to meet the responsibilities ahead without a clue how to meet them? Had he ever had the strength for this? He knew he had—of course he had—but how?

He wasn't aware of how it happened, but he found himself holding a file folder, then sinking into the gap between the file cabinet and the bookshelf. Down there it smelled of school in a nasty way—old flooring, old metal, old dust, musty paper. He was paralyzed, unable to act or imagine acting; he didn't recognize himself or fathom his next task.

Was this what they called *cowering*? Was this it, crouching in fear, hiding from reach, unable to get up, move forward, stop being a *coward*?

"Are you okay?"

He was a big kid, black, probably a senior, standing over him.

"It's nothing." Luke snapped out of the stupor of his paralysis and held up the folder. "I was just retrieving this."

The kid offered a hand, helping Luke to his feet. "Glad I found you, Mr. Devlin. Counselor told me to get your signature.

I just wanted to get into your Twentieth Century History class, fifth hour. I'm a senior, and I don't need the social studies credit, so it'll be an elective. I just like history."

The kid waved a printed form as Luke, still red-faced, propped himself on the edge of his desk and took the paperwork, pretending to study it. "I've got to check that hour. I'm not sure if I have any space."

"You do. My counselor and I just checked. It's like your one opening all day. And I'm not ass kissing, Mr. Devlin. I really am a history freak. I'm hoping to major in American studies."

"American studies. Yeah! A great major. My pulse beats a little faster when I think of history and culture together like that."

"I heard you teach that way. Bringing in literature and art and music. Philosophy, even. My friend Shan'Telle, who took the class last year? Said you weren't bad."

"Shan'Telle Washington? She's not bad, either. I love that girl."

"That makes two of us."

The big senior reminded Luke of his brother. An African American Matthew Devlin at seventeen. It was the wondrous company of another human being completely at home in his own skin and inviting you to come on over and hang close for while.

"Well, please tell Shan'Telle I miss her."

Luke heard a chuckle in the doorway, the jangle of bracelets, and then a familiar face leaning into the doorway, laughing now as she approached the desk. "It's my fault, Mr. Devlin." She held hands with the kid. "I knew he could sweet-talk you into taking one more student."

Suddenly it flooded back, Shan'Telle's year-end presentation, a brooding, angry, and funny examination of whether the word *nigger* should be banned or revised in earlier documents and literature, with lots of spicy research on the word's etymology and troublemaking across the century. "Shan'Telle set a new standard for student presentations last year. The bar is raised higher now, are you really up for it?" he asked the big kid.

"I'll vouch for him," Shan'Telle said, pulling at the boy's arm. Then she reversed course and leaned in to buss Luke on the cheek. "And I love you, too, Mr. Devlin."

❖

August 28

I was feeling much better after seeing Shan'Telle and getting ready for the coming week. I had no idea Emily had any acquaintance with my surprise visitor—how'd they get together to set up that wonderful ambush? I started down the front steps of the school, ready to walk home with a pack full of books and articles when this guy called to me from the curb.

It was Jeff Douglas, dressed in office costume himself—slacks and a tie. He looked so good, smiling so wide, but it just revived months' worth of resentment and turmoil. He asked if he could walk me home, joked about carrying my books. I said I couldn't stop him from walking, it's a free country, but I could carry my own pack.

So he kept pace with me, walking at my side while blurting it all out. He implored me to listen—as if I weren't hanging on every vowel and consonant, afraid we'd run out of blocks to cross before he finished his tale and I shut the door in his face. Those weren't his kids, but a visiting relative's, playing on the ranch house lawn. He and Cassie didn't have any children. And Cassie had wanted a divorce for many months, but he'd been trying to avoid a battle with her family, who owned the ranch, over his share of the property and business. He was only technically married when he met me. They'd been estranged for a long time. Now that the divorce was going through, he was severing his interest in the Wyoming ranch and working full-time for the Cattlemen's Association. He was just moving into his own place in Denver, a condo on Little Raven Street in the riverfront. He could walk over the Millennium Bridge to his office in Lower Downtown.

Mighty urban and swanky for a damn cowboy. Ex-cowboy. If it was all true, why hadn't he just told me from the beginning? Why all the secretive BS?

By now we were at my parents' front porch. I felt like I was living the high school romance traumas I'd been spared when I was a solitary gay geek in high school. I stopped at the bottom steps to keep him from coming any closer. He understood and kept on the sidewalk, telling me that back in June, he couldn't give Cassie or her family's lawyers any opportunity to mess up his reputation. It wasn't a case of trying to have an affair on the side or keep anything in the closet. It was a case of meeting me at the wrong time, because he really did fall in love with me.

He said the thing that gave him hope whenever I hung up or deleted his texts was that none of his messages had ever bounced back, so he knew I hadn't blocked him or erased him as a contact.

I couldn't explain that. Just an oversight? A subconscious desire to reconnect? It's too exhausting to consider right now. I told him I would give it some thought, but I don't know how to begin thinking, my family's going through some trouble right now.

"Emily and Gail told me," he said. "I threw myself at their mercy and told them everything. They told me everything, too. I'm so sorry for what you and your family have been through. I'm sorry my timing is always so bad. But I can still offer you my company, my shoulder, my solace. Wouldn't it be better to try to be friends again than going it alone and staying angry over a misunderstanding?"

I told him I would call when I was ready and went inside. I didn't know how to answer or what to believe. I still don't. I'm writing this a bit too late anyway. I'm on the patio, using up the reverse sides of this used-up summer journal. It's breezy, a bit cool, darkness has fallen and the crickets are clacking like crazy. I have to hit the sack. It's a school night.

❖

Luke began to enjoy having family dinners regularly, every evening during the first week of school. He was going to miss them when he went back to whatever junky one bedroom he could afford anywhere near the central city. With Jenn and Kathy bustling in the kitchen while Ted insisted men were better cooks, they let him make the marinara sauce until it dawned on him that it was the Tom Sawyer whitewash-the-fence trick, and the women laughed, a wonderful sound to hear in the kitchen again.

But their laughter died quickly, and all of them went off

separately to their rooms after dinner. A ferocious silence would grip the house while Luke juggled his lesson plans and the next draft of his Summitville thesis for Buster. He again felt the disquiet those solitary gaps of time in the summer after he'd lost Jeff Douglas and before he began to lose his brother.

❖

Thursday night, he texted Jeff. *Get together for dinner later in Sept OK? Anywhere but that Indian place.*
Jeff texted back *OK!*

❖

Friday evening, when the preparations for the memorial were finally done, the four Vine Street housemates gathered on the back patio, relaxing with wine and beer in the early twilight cool down. Jenn asked Ted'n'Kathy about the status of the Ecuadorian wildlands.

Ted made it clear the government's decision to sell drilling rights in the preserve would be their ruination. "Our research started as a hopeful hedge against development," Ted said. "To produce evidence of the preserve's immense value to the Ecuadorian government as wild land. But once the rights were sold, our work changed to cataloguing what will probably be lost."

"Forever," Kathy sighed, swirling her wine.

"I keep wondering," Jenn said, sighing herself. "What if you knew who really underwrites the Clean Energy Council?" Jenn said. "I found out for sure on our filming shoot in Pennsylvania. It's the same corporation that's going to destroy what your research tried to save. It's the exact same royal Dutch petroleum conglomerate plowing under your Ecuadorian enclave. That's who's really writing my paychecks. Now do you see why I had to take some to think alone about where my life and career were heading, minus Matt? Plus, the baby."

"It's too much, Jenn, too much to absorb all at once and keep your equilibrium," Kathy said. "Anyway, I can see why you've made such an impact. You really are great in those commercials, funny and sincere."

"But sincere about what? At first, I was naïve. I accepted the Clean Energy Council at face value. Yet I knew, I really knew, and denied it to myself. I wanted that contract. I wanted that money. I wanted to project my talent out there."

"We're all culpable," Luke said. "Every one of us who drives a car or catches a flight or flips a switch."

"You have a contract to fulfill," Ted said. "But then it's over, correct?"

"You know how Clean Energy's production company reacted when I raised the question of getting out of my contract? They offered to pay me more. That's how they think. I'm just hesitating because I want a bigger cut. They're making so much off this fake Vanessa and her loyal following. It's such a public relations coup, they want to move up the fall schedule so they can make the new Colorado ad series before I start showing. Then, later, they want to shoot a new series, Pregnant Vanessa, plucking at America's heartstrings with her baby-to-be and the wondrous future of fossil fuels."

"We trust you to make the right decision, Jenn," Ted said. "But it sounds to me like they really need Vanessa now. That gives you clout, even after you've honored your contract. Imagine if Vanessa herself shows up at a climate conference with a more honest message about the real costs of fossil fuels."

"And remember," Kathy said, "we'll support your decisions. You can rent or sell the condo. You can hire a new manager for the shop or sell the business. We're not going back to Ecuador until well after the new year, if ever. We'd love to have you stay here, living with us. If you decide to keep the baby, we'd love to help you through it. I won't pretend it wouldn't thrill me to have a grandchild." Kathy clasped her hands together. "And, Luke, will you stay, too? I won't beg you, and I know you're ready to get another place of your own. But if you would stay with us, maybe through the holidays, I would love it. We'll be a houseful again, a family, instead of two heartbroken geeks knocking into each other in a lonely old Denver square."

SEPTEMBER

Sept 3

I took off alone the day after the memorial, the Sunday before Labor Day, almost five hours down US 285, then straight south to Alamosa, where I planned to stage my own investigation into the scene of the crime. Summitville mine.

The drive through vast open spaces, the gorgeous summits surrounding South Park, and then along the Sangre de Cristos and Sawatch Range through the San Luis Valley, was like a pure tonic to clear my mind. The memorial on Saturday, as homey and informal as we tried to make it, had packed the parish center with so many people I expected and didn't expect and had half forgotten. The later arrivals had to stand on the front sidewalk in a passing thunderstorm, straining to listen to the loudspeakers in the foyer. After them came Matt's schoolmates from way back in catechism and the sacraments and elementary and middle and high school, Matt's schoolteachers and coaches and teammates and hiking, biking, skiing, and river buddies and ex-girlfriends and all their spouses and all their kids. Each face unfolded into doors upon doors of memories, outdoor adventures and school shenanigans. I could hardly bear the eulogy, eloquent and funny and torturously sad, delivered by the same priest who had confirmed Matt and obviously did his homework on his life in the seventeen years since.

When the priest offered the podium to the immediate family, my folks politely declined. Mom, for the first time, looked crushed, physically unable to rise from her front-row seat. I sat between Jenn and Emily, holding each by the hand, squeezing for dear life, unable and unwilling to go anywhere near that podium. I love words, but sometimes they are useless to capture a universe of silent, roiling feeling. I wasn't even gonna try. We heard a score of touching personal tributes from well-spoken extroverts and brave introverts at the podium and then, oh God, a whole afternoon and evening with the relatives at home, an alcohol-fueled wake full of heartfelt connections and sentimental recollections. I woke with a start at sunrise and filled a trash bag with the wake's waste, hauled the cans to the recycling bin, then left a note about my getaway stuck to the fridge and got away.

We get to do it all again next Saturday in Fruita, but the picnic in the park should be quite a bit less intense. Jenn says the big event is going to be a balloon release and the main dish grilled tofu dogs.

Right now I'm writing on Sunday evening on the patio of a good little coffee shop in Alamosa. This great couple from Rio Guardians, whom I'd contacted when I was researching my thesis and just before this trip, insisted I stay at their place and gave me pointers and orientation about visiting the mine, two and a half hours west of here.

They're excited by Buster Levine's offer to help me publish my research and, with more notice, willing to give me a weekend tour of the whole watershed around Summitville and share their findings on contaminate flows. We'd need advance permission to enter the Superfund site from the main entrance. They've got two little kids at home, but it's supremely quiet compared to a houseful of my relatives, and I'm loving the break from memorializing, not to mention half-consciously expecting Matt to reappear around every corner of our house and garden. Blame it on too many beers, but late last night I actually turned from a group of cousins and checked to see where Matt had gone.

Having the whole drive then this evening to myself has even given me a little breathing space to think about Jeff. I was disgusted with myself that I was so elated to see him last Monday, so lured by his I-love-yous, and still so attracted. I thought I'd moved past all that, especially in the throes of this insanely busy, stressful, and grief-stricken week, but no. I have the same Pavlovian response to love, the same animal desire, no matter how I've tried to resist. And damn it, he is funnier, smarter, tougher, and yet more tender than the four thousand other guys I've dated since high school. I'm glad I decided to message him.

On the highway this morning, I listened to a public radio interview with a Buddhist philosopher who discussed the key tenet of detachment. I always have trouble wrapping my consciousness around that, a philosophy based on compassion that advocates detachment. The philosopher said she welcomed opportunities to learn about suffering. She mentioned the cruel fate of zoo animals left behind in a Middle Eastern city wracked by years of civil war, viewing the news of their abandonment, their thirsting and starving to death alone in their cages, as an opportunity to practice compassion through detachment.

I suppose that's better than freaking out, railing against it hopelessly, and crying out in despair. But isn't Sartre's approach of taking action more effective? Why not send money, contact animal rescue, or protest the neglect instead of indulging the Buddhists' serene detachment and private practice of compassion? What good is compassion without action?

Yet it's not like Sartre's existential isolation impresses me, either. I just can't stop thinking about that opposing concept of attachment, not as a desperate clinging to people, material goods, and sentimental habits, or even being stuck in place, but as a healthy response to the complexity of our environments and the depth of our relationships.

At Matt's hospital bedside, I reread one of his favorites, *The Catcher in the Rye*, and was struck by an irony I'd never noticed, how Holden starts off his story mocking all that "David Copperfield crap." He's too cool for that, but then he proceeds to narrate an entire novel about how his escape from boarding school home to the city pulls him back into David Copperfieldian attachments, all of it flowing from the wellspring of grief for his brother.

When I was a teenager, I once served as an unpaid assistant on one of Ted's summer research projects in the Snowy Range west of Laramie, Wyoming. After morning stints of searching for a rare montane skipper, we had lots of downtime in a vast, empty national forest campground. Our camp connected to the banks of a sparkling little stream, more tranquil than the rowdy whitewater tumble of most Colorado high country creeks. I took my camp chair to the sunny bank and read *David Copperfield*—at Judith's suggestion—in great gulps. Afterward with Judith's guidance I realized *David Copperfield* isn't the crappy, tired classic I expected but a massive Victorian fictional autobiography that according to her was "a miracle of organization by theme, and that theme is human attachment, pure and simple, a subject we never give its due."

I got it, thinking back. David gets so attached to family and friends that attachment itself is the book's binding agent. It might be the remedy to existential isolation, our aloneness transformed into joyous connection. What the hell is wrong with that, Holden? And what about you, ghoulish Buddhist lady?

I pretty much followed the Alamosa River up to the mine. The flat valley ended where a bridge crossed into a ghostly, abandoned ranch along the river, empty paneless windows peering out on pasture gone to weeds. I inspected the healthy trees lining the banks and noted the bugless, birdless silence of the fast-moving water itself. Higher up, here and there an aspen already slipped from green to gold. The road rose into a typical, healthy-looking Colorado alpine valley, a spruce and fir paradise under steep slopes.

Past a deserted, locked-up fishing camp, the road split, the narrow, steeper grade heading over oddly dry, red ochre streambeds. My Rio Guardian hosts had coached me to stop here to find a faint trail beside a tributary of Bitter Creek and hike a few rough miles up to the mine's unguarded backside.

I could not understand the ruined, thirsty gash of the former streambed, choked with gravel-like pebbles and huge boulders. Where had the water gone in this snow-melting, rainy zone, this tumbling, rocky fountain of a mountainside? The banks still bled rust-red from oxide, but how did the dusty dried-blood powder survive decades of snows and storms?

Hiking beside it for a couple hours, I felt like the last glob of hemoglobin coursing up the dead, silenced artery of a mountain-sized bloodstream. The trail eventually led away from the streambed into a fir forest that had died off tree by tree, from dark green evergreen canopies to stark sticks, blackened not by fire but slow mortality. Eventually every tree was a dead sentinel, sparser and sparser as I approached the summit. From the grass-tufted, barren top of the rim, after all my intimate research in libraries and computers, I viewed the Summitville mine for the first time. Unsteady on the ridge's edge, I stared into the pit, stunned.

In all my examination of evidence in photographs and description in reports, nothing prepared me for the scale of the real thing. "The worst-conceived, worst-operated, and worst-designed mine in the history of mining," in the words of a local official. Clawing into the red-stained mountain ridge to the west, a great crude scoop appeared. An ochre-brown wound slashed fake canyon walls as if the children of heedless giants had played at digging in the sand, then abandoned their game in mid-scrape. Only it was nothing like a sandbox. Behind the aborted line of trees, the great granite peaks once rose to thirteen thousand feet to form the Great Divide, the magnificent summits this old mine was named for, summits clawed away to gouge this vast abyss in the earth.

In the 1980s, the Canadian fortune hunters who acquired, raped, and abandoned it were after the most basic goal of acquisitiveness—the glory of all Gollums—gold, acquired by leaching it from ore with cyanide. The toxic brew still soured here, stretching under me for a thousand acres, barely contained, depositing heavy metals into the tributaries of the upper Rio Grande, most of which are eventually ingested, trapped and swelling without remedy in human bodies, especially the youngest ones. The corporate Canadians declared bankruptcy and walked away. Good God, what were such people ever attached to besides gold? Not our continent, not our earth, not our children.

I hiked past a stream bubbling out of the containment structures, so I went back down bearing still-empty containers, to where Bitter Creek itself looked like a normal Rocky Mountain stream, roaring through a piney chasm. I took water samples to satisfy my own curiosity; Dad could help me analyze the contaminants with a valid methodology. On a rocky ledge over the creek, I watched the furious rivulets roil southwestward, where they would join the Alamosa River and eventually empty into the Rio Grande, still discharging a trace of its poisons all the way to the Gulf of Mexico. From my research, I remembered the worst toxic overflows in the early 1990s. Seventy miles of the Alamosa River were polluted to point of killing most aquatic life. Experts estimated it would take a hundred years or more to restore.

A hundred years, longer than most human lives. Beside the creek, I felt enfolded in the ethical approaches to the disaster I had tried to analyze from Denver. Here, they weren't ideas, they were cubic flows per minute at my feet.

I thought of what Matt, blissed out on the Colorado River canyons, told me that day in June, how rivers ought to be worshipped as tangible, earthly gods. My agreement makes me just as bad an existentialist as I was a Catholic because I put one essence before existence, that of the living earth. I was perfectly prepared to accept the essential reality of Mother Earth as a sentient, purposeful organism. A goddess. Of course, we could keep treating our waterways as sewers, the flush option for our waste, our poisons and toxins, and contaminate other lives downstream. Maybe Matt was just being descriptive, not romantic, when he said that rivers were sacred, their courses parallel to human lives, which after all are ambulatory waterways coursing in capillaries. We share the same hurried current. We can only go forward, ever growing but oblivious from our small, seeping beginnings, slipping past obstacles of greed and deceit. Our time on earth seemed to me shorter than ever, brotherless, a sneeze in eternity, a contaminated absurdity.

Here in Alamosa, the night before Labor Day, it's time to end this poor tattered journal. First thing tomorrow, I'll hit the road for the long drive home. Summer's over.

About the Author

A native of California's Mendocino Coast, Lee Patton has enjoyed life in Colorado since college. His fiction and poetry have been widely published and his plays produced nationwide. His novels include *Nothing Gold Can Stay*, a Lambda Literary Award finalist; *Love and Genetic Weaponry*; and *My Aim Is True*. *Faith of Power*, a novella, is featured in Main Street Rag's 2017 anthology, *In the Middle*. He received an MA in fiction from the University of Denver's Writing Program.

Books Available From Bold Strokes Books

Every Summer Day by Lee Patton. Meant to celebrate every summer day, Luke's journal instead chronicles a love affair as fast-moving and possibly as fatal as his brother's brain tumor. (978-1-63555-706-0)

Everyday People by Louis Barr. When film star Diana Danning hires private eye Clint Steele to find her son, Clint turns to his former West Point barracks mate, and ex-buddy with benefits, Mars Hauser to lend his cyber espionage and digital black ops skills to the case.(978-1-63555-698-8)

Cirque des Freaks and Other Tales of Horror by Julian Lopez. Explore the pleasure of horror in this compilation that delivers like the horror classics…good ole tales of terror. (978-1-63555-689-6)

Royal Street Reveillon by Greg Herren. In this Scotty Bradley mystery, someone is killing the stars of a reality show, and it's up to Scotty Bradley and the boys to find out who. (978-1-63555-545-5)

Death Takes a Bow by David S. Pederson. Alan Keys takes part in a local stage production, but when the leading man is murdered, his partner Detective Heath Barrington is thrust into the limelight to find the killer. (978-1-63555-472-4)

Accidental Prophet by Bud Gundy. Days after his grandmother dies, Drew Morten learns his true identity and finds himself racing against time to save civilization from the apocalypse. (978-1-63555-452-6)

In Case You Forgot by Fredrick Smith and Chaz Lamar. Zaire and Kenny, two newly single, Black, queer, and socially aware men, start again—in love, career, and life—in the West Hollywood neighborhood of LA. (978-1-63555-493-9)

Counting for Thunder by Phillip Irwin Cooper. A struggling actor returns to the Deep South to manage a family crisis but finds love and ultimately his own voice as his mother is regaining hers for possibly the last time. (978-1-63555-450-2)

Survivor's Guilt and Other Stories by Greg Herren. Award-winning author Greg Herren's short stories are finally pulled together into a single collection, including the Macavity Award–nominated title story and the first-ever Chanse MacLeod short story. (978-1-63555-413-7)

Saints + Sinners Anthology 2019, edited by Tracy Cunningham and Paul Willis. An anthology of short fiction featuring the finalist selections from the 2019 Saints + Sinners Literary Festival. (978-1-63555-447-2)

The Shape of the Earth by Gary Garth McCann. After appearing in *Best Gay Love Stories*, *HarringtonGMFQ*, *Q Review*, and *Off the Rocks*, Lenny and his partner Dave return in a hotbed of manhood and jealousy. (978-1-63555-391-8)

Exit Plans for Teenage Freaks by 'Nathan Burgoine. Cole always has a plan—especially for escaping his small-town reputation as "that kid who was kidnapped when he was four"—but when he teleports to a museum, it's time to face facts: it's possible he's a total freak after all. (978-1-163555-098-6)

Death Checks In by David S. Pederson. Despite Heath's promises to Alan to not get involved, Heath can't resist investigating a shopkeeper's murder in Chicago, which dashes their plans for a romantic weekend getaway. (978-1-163555-329-1)

Of Echoes Born by 'Nathan Burgoine. A collection of queer fantasy short stories set in Canada from Lambda Literary Award finalist 'Nathan Burgoine. (978-1-63555-096-2)

The Lurid Sea by Tom Cardamone. Cursed to spend eternity on his knees, Nerites is having the time of his life. (978-1-62639-911-2)

Sinister Justice by Steve Pickens. When a vigilante targets citizens of Jake Finnigan's hometown, Jake and his partner Sam fall under suspicion themselves as they investigate the murders. (978-1-63555-094-8)

Club Arcana: Operation Janus by Jon Wilson. Wizards, demons, Elder Gods: Who knew the universe was so crowded, and that they'd all be out to get Angus McAslan? (978-1-62639-969-3)

Triad Soul by 'Nathan Burgoine. Luc, Anders, and Curtis—vampire, demon, and wizard—must use their powers of blood, soul, and magic to defeat a murderer determined to turn their city into a battlefield. (978-1-62639-863-4)